DREAMS OF THE WOLF

The Gray Pack #4

LORI KING

BLURB

The Gray Pack 4
   Dreams of the Wolf

Katie-Jo (KJ) Whetstone is on a mission to save her mother's life and protect the Quiver Creek pack from Nicolas Kaplan, a deranged werewolf. She has already journeyed across the country from Wyoming to Missouri to find brothers that she never knew, and now she must lead them back against their own reservations. She's shocked when her libido goes haywire over the only human traveling with them, Dr. Thomas Jameson.

Fighting to keep her distance from the mating lust, KJ and Thomas both end up needing to be rescued. Bryson Samuels is an enemy wolf that makes her body sing as loudly as Thomas does. With strangers for mates, she fights the need to bond, with her desire to be free from the pack. In the end they will all have to decide if they are willing to do anything to protect each other.

For Lisa and Chris, who keep me focused on the end goal, while always making me laugh. I couldn't ask for two bigger supporters.
And for my husband—you are my dream come true.
I hope to always Live, Laugh, and Love like today is my only chance.
Always~Lori

PROLOGUE

From her place on the front porch of the Alpha's cabin, KJ watched as her brothers said their good-byes to their new wife, Shandi. In just a few brief moments they would all be gathering their stuff and loading up in the black SUVs that lined the driveway. Their destination was Quiver Creek, Wyoming, and their goal was to help bring her parents back to the Gray Pack den.

KJ's heart ached with sadness, as Ryley and Shandi both waved at her and smiled, while Rafe glared daggers in her direction. Instead of returning their friendly gesture, she rolled her eyes and turned away. There was no point in getting to know these people. She wouldn't be sticking around here. Once Mom and Dad were settled in with the Gray Pack, she would be free to set out on her own. There would be no one to tell her when she could come and go, no rationing of food and supplies, and no male rogues threatening her with a possible mating. Katie Jo Whetstone would finally be able to be her own person.

Walking through the Alpha's cabin into the kitchen, she was brought up short as the sexiest man she had ever seen came sauntering in from the kitchen. His eyes were a dark muddy brown, and his equally dark brown hair was cut neatly to match his perfectly groomed mustache and goatee. Lean but muscular, KJ guessed he stood at least six foot two. Her head would tuck perfectly under his chin, and against his firm chest. Shaking herself hard, her eyes widened as his scent filled her nostrils, and her wolf began howling in her head.

Panic gripped her chest, and her lungs constricted. This stranger was her mate. There was no other explanation for this kind of reaction. *No,* she thought to herself as she jerked her gaze away from the sinfully good-looking man, *I can't have a mate yet, I have to find myself first.*

The stranger chose that moment to turn his head and meet her gaze. She could feel his eyes drifting down her body, and a red flush crept up her throat and cheeks. He brought his head back up and their eyes locked. Just that fraction of a second made her knees tremble, and her pussy clench. His pupils dilated as his body reacted to its perfect mate, and she swallowed hard when he took a step in her direction.

Without a second thought, she spun on her heel and ran for the front door. She pushed past Damon Gray who was coming in from the other side and left a wide berth between her and her new brothers. She couldn't handle family time right now. As she shot into the woods, she instinctively shifted into her wolf form, feeling her clothing rip away from her body, as she landed on four paws.

As always, the smell of the earth was coupled with the fragrance of the trees, and she breathed deeply trying to clear her brain. Her mate. That's who the stranger was. It was the only reason for her wolf to go this haywire based on his scent alone.

She ran for a few more moments, before she slowed to an easy canter, and then dropped to her belly in the middle of a clearing. After a few more blissful moments of solitude she heard the sounds of wolves behind her. Rafe, Ryley, and Shandi all burst forward in wolf form, coming to an abrupt stop in front of her.

Shifting into their human skin, Shandi and Ryley shared a glance before moving cautiously toward her. KJ shifted into her human form, and planted her hands on her hips giving them an angry glare.

"Why did you follow me?"

Ryley's hands went up as if to hold her off, and he shook his head. "Whoa there, tiger. You looked upset."

"So?" Maybe they were actually concerned about her.

"We just wanted to make sure you were okay, KJ," Shandi said softly from where she had stopped a few feet away.

KJ stared at her new sister-in-law in amazement, and then movement caught her attention as Rafe shifted into his human skin.

"Come on. She's clearly fine," he snapped at Shandi and Ryley who both looked torn between following his orders and comforting her.

"Rafe—" Shandi started, but KJ held her hand up.

"I got upset because the cabin was too full of people. I don't like crowds. I needed some space," KJ said staring into her big brother's eyes. The glacial blue orbs narrowed in on her, and he shook his head.

"Bullshit," he said, refusing to release her gaze.

Shock rippled through her. "Excuse me?"

"I call bullshit on you. Something more than a crowded cabin happened to you, but if that's how you want to spin it," he said, shifting his weight onto his heels as he crossed both arms in front of his massive chest.

KJ turned her head into the soft breeze as she processed his words. She wanted desperately to come clean and tell him that she had just stumbled into her soul mate, but if anyone knew, they would push the two of them together. She just needed some time to process it before she introduced herself to the man fate wanted her to spend the rest of her life with.

Turning back to the trio, she shrugged. "What do you care?"

Ryley and Shandi both groaned as a smirk spread over Rafe's face. "I don't care, but my mate does. If she wants you happy, then I'll do my damnedest to keep her happy."

"No one needs to worry about me. I've been taking care of myself for years," KJ said, trying to ignore the tightness in her chest.

"But now you have a whole pack of family to help you," Shandi said.

KJ barked out a laugh, "No, I don't. I thought that maybe there was a chance I would find a family here, but that was a hopeless bit of optimism. Instead, I found doubt and anger, not to mention ridicule."

"What?" Ryley snarled, and KJ stared at him in silent shock. "What the hell do you mean ridicule? Who's fucking with you?"

The sting of tears in her eyes irritated KJ as she swallowed hard trying to control her reaction to his protectiveness. "It doesn't matter. All that matters is that I know my place around here. I need your help saving our mother's life. If we don't figure out what's wrong with her soon, she will probably die."

"We're already leaving our brand-new wife to come save the day for your parents, what more do you want from us?" Rafe asked nastily.

KJ grimaced and spewed out the first words on her tongue. "They are your parents, too."

"That remains to be proven." Rafe's tone was ice cold, and KJ shivered.

"Whatever look I'm not going to debate it with you. It's as clear as the raised eyebrow on your face that I'm your sister, but if you need to see them to prove it, well, your wish is my command. You'll be eating your words in a matter of days," KJ said angrily.

"Stop it, right now. Both of you. Rafe, you and I both know she's our blood, even if you're too hardheaded to admit it right now. Why don't you and Shandi go for a quick run before we leave, and I'll go back to the cabin with KJ. She needs to meet Thomas, and I think he's there with Tina now," Ryley said.

KJ, Rafe, and Shandi all gaped at him, before Shandi started laughing. "Well now I've seen everything. Ryley Whetstone, since when did you become the serious one?"

Ryley's trademark cheeky grin lifted his lips, and KJ found herself smiling back. The only one left frowning was Rafe.

"I'll be there in ten, Ry," Rafe said, before he dropped down to the ground in wolf form and padded off into the woods. Shandi shifted with a shake of her head and a heavy sigh, and followed him, leaving KJ alone with Ryley.

"Do you have to antagonize him?" Ryley asked.

"I don't appreciate being called a liar."

Ryley cursed under his breath. "You have to understand our side of it too. You've had your parents for your whole life. Our parents left us, remember? Without a good-bye, or an explanation, they just left. I told you before that it's going to be the hardest on Rafe, can't you just go easy on him?"

KJ felt pointedly admonished and hated the feeling. "So you think this is easy on me? I've grown up hearing about how perfect my two older brothers were and seeing the sorrow in my mother's eyes every time she talked about you guys. How, someday we were going to go back and get you, or join you or something, anything, just to be a whole family. When I finally get the chance to meet you, one of you turns out to be a douche bag."

Ryley's face was a dark shade of red, and a small muscle in his jaw ticked with tension. "Fine. We're all struggling with our emotions, but that doesn't mean we have to be at each other's throats. Try to give him some space while we're on this trip, otherwise he's likely to rip yours out."

With that Ryley shifted into his wolf and cocked his head like he was waiting for her to do the same. With another pointed eye roll and a huffy sigh, she shifted and followed him back to the Alpha's cabin.

The moment they reached the tree line they both shifted and continued on foot. Ryley greeted several people as they went into the cabin, but KJ stayed silent, heading directly toward her bag that was still sitting next to the stairs. She pulled out a pair of jeans and a T-shirt, and was just settling the fabric over her naked breasts as the spicy scent of man hit her nose.

Her eyes drifted shut, and she inhaled deeply. For just a moment her head spun and her body swayed as she was swamped with the sensation of her mate's nearness. Two hands settled softly on her shoulders as if to steady her, and a deep, rich voice broke through her lusty haze.

"Are you all right, little one?"

Her eyes shot open and locked onto the deep brown of his. Electricity zipped through her system, and all the air expelled from her lungs as he inhaled sharply. His gaze darkened with desire, just as he jerked his hands away from her.

The man cleared his throat and shoved his hands in his jeans pockets. "Are you all right? You looked like you were going to pass out."

KJ swallowed hard and opened her mouth to speak, but the only sound that escaped her throat was a soft, sensual growl…

CHAPTER ONE

*E*arlier in the week...

"I'm tired, Tink. I've been working fourteen hours a day at the wound care clinic for the last four years, and I'm not sure that it's even what I want to be doing." Thomas spoke into the phone, as he lounged in his favorite La-Z-Boy recliner. The blue fabric was worn and frayed on the armrests, and the footrest was slightly lopsided, but it was more comfortable than anywhere else on Earth for him these days.

"Then why are you still doing it?" The simple question from his little sister made him laugh, but he couldn't answer it.

That was the problem. Thomas Jameson didn't know exactly why he was still fumbling through every day with no real purpose, and he honestly had no clue how to change the direction of his life. At thirty-two years old, he had made a niche for himself as a doctor, but it wasn't the niche that he wanted to be in. He had always assumed that he would have a wife and children by now, but instead he spent the few hours of personal time he had sitting in his comfy chair with his laptop in hand, or the TV on. It was existing but not living, and he was ready for changes.

"Well I could live off my trust fund...Oh wait, that's right I don't have one. I'm not independently wealthy, Tink. I have to have a job to pay my bills. Including the fifty thousand or so I have in student loan debt," he said, resigned to his fate in the everyday drudgery of general wound care.

"What if I had a job opportunity for you?" Tina's voice sounded hopeful, but Thomas was rolling his eyes. She had been pestering him to come and work for the same hospital she did for a while now. It was always the same song and dance, and he wasn't interested. He just didn't see himself working in a large hospital. He hated the bureaucratic bullshit, the coworker gossip, and the constant pissing matches between resident doctors. It just wasn't the life he wanted.

"I'm not interested in working for St. Leonard's, Tink," he started to say with a sigh.

"I didn't say anything about you working for Leo's. I said I had a job opportunity for you. Look, you are the only human that knows about the Gray Pack, and it just so happens that the pack needs a doctor as quickly as possible."

Now she had his attention. He put his footrest down so he could sit up. The werewolf pack that his sister had become a part of when she met her fiancé, Liam, was a source of perpetual intrigue for him. He had only met a few of the members of the pack so far, but he liked the ones he knew, and they took care of his little sister as though she had been born into their family. He had so many questions as a doctor, about what happened physiologically when they shifted into their wolf form, and even more questions about how their society worked.

The pack leader, Devin, had been courteous and friendly, but had not been particularly forthcoming with information, so Thomas was in the dark for the most part. He had spent many nights awake in his bed running various questions through his head and wondering if he would ever have the answers to them. Now Tina was giving him the opportunity to work amongst them and treat them as patients. It was almost too good to be true.

"What's the catch?"

She growled low in her throat, and he grinned at the standard Tina reaction. "Why would you assume there is a catch, big brother?"

"Because, my darling Tink, nothing good happens in my world. I have learned that every good thing comes with a kick in the gut. Now, what's the catch?"

"They need you here by this coming Sunday, and you'll be traveling to Wyoming with part of the pack."

A surge of excitement ran the length of his body, and he swallowed hard. "This Sunday?"

"Yeah, do you remember Rafe and Ryley? The two blond guys who came over to your place with us when Cash got shot?" she asked.

A memory of twin blond mountains with enormous shoulders, and movie star smiles flashed in his brain. "They looked a little like Vikings, right? Yeah, I remember them."

"Okay, well, they were actually adopted into the Gray Pack when they were little kids. Their parents brought them here, and then disappeared leaving them behind. No one was ever able to find any trace of them. Then yesterday, we got a surprise visitor to the den, and it turns out that she is Rafe and Ryley's little sister, Katie Jo Whetstone, KJ for short. Their parents have been on the run from a really bad dude for years, and they left their kids here because they thought it would be safer. They managed to find a hiding place and set up a den, but Nicolas Kaplan found them and has been pestering them. Now that they are getting older, they can't keep running anymore, and they asked for help from Devin. The problem is that they've collected a bunch of rogue wolves and formed a little mini pack up in Wyoming. They have asked us to help get them back to our den, and they want Devin to take them in as members of the Gray Pack."

"Is Devin really willing to take them all in without meeting them?"

Tina sighed. "Yeah, it seems so. I don't think he's promised them all acceptance into the pack, but he has promised our assistance in getting them out of Quiver Creek. According to KJ if we don't get them out of there, Nicolas's wolves will end up capturing or killing them off one by one."

"So why do you need a doctor?"

"Apparently, Tasha Whetstone, Rafe, Ryley, and KJ's mom, has been shot recently in the arm, and it isn't healing. She suspects that the bullet was silver, or silver laced. Silver is toxic to a werewolf in certain doses. They need her to be seen by a doctor, but they can't risk taking her to a human hospital. That's where you come in."

Thomas's brain was on overload, and he closed his eyes while he thought through all that Tina had just said. "So they only need me temporarily?"

"No, actually that was something else…um…you see, I'm going to be turning in my resignation to St. Leo's because we're going to open a permanent medical clinic here at the den. We need to have something available for injuries and illnesses, so we don't have to drag people into Kansas City all the time and risk questions. I want you to work with me to open the clinic and stay on as the pack doctor. Devin said that they will match your current salary—"

"I'm in." He heard himself respond, and it surprised both of them. The only thing he had was his gut instinct, but something told him that this was the direction he was supposed to go. Hadn't he just been asking God what was next for him? *Well here's your sign, genius,* he thought to himself with a grin.

Tina was silent for a moment as though she was shocked by his response. "Really?"

"Hell yes, I'm in. You're offering me a chance to leave the job I have, that's become monotonous and irritating, and I will get to treat *werewolves.* I'll turn in my resignation tomorrow." The excitement in his belly was nearly overwhelming. He wanted to jump up and down and scream with it, but instead he calmly waited for Tina's response.

"Thank you, Tommy! You're a lifesaver! Now, Devin said that if you agreed to be the pack doctor they would make sure you had a house here to move into, but you can wait until you get back to pack up and move if you want." Tina was bubbling over with enthusiasm, and Thomas couldn't hold back a chuckle.

"Slow down, Tink, I have a couple more questions. How long are they expecting this trip to Wyoming to take? And who all is coming along?"

"Hopefully not long—a couple weeks at most. Rafe and Ryley are obviously going, and KJ is leading the way. Then Cash, the one that you treated when he got shot, and his brother Owen are going too. You'll like him, he's an attorney. I'm pretty sure that another pair of brothers, Noah and Luke, will be going as well. So, it will be the eight of you."

"So everyone else that is going is a werewolf, right?"

"Yes, but don't worry, you won't be left behind, human. They are planning on taking a couple big fifteen passenger vans, so they have something to use to transport the new wolves back in," she said playfully, and he grunted at her.

"You were human until just recently if I recall, Tink."

"Yes, but now I'm so much more, and so much better, don't you think?"

"I see that humility didn't come with your new fur coat." He rolled his eyes to the ceiling. Tina wasn't the type to bite her tongue. She always said whatever popped into her head, and he loved her for it. In a world of people who said one thing, but meant another, she was a breath of fresh air.

"Who needs humility when you can run like the wind and look gorgeous while doing it?" she said flippantly. "Anyway, I better get off here, and call Devin to let him know you're taking the job. Can you plan on being at my place Sunday?"

"I actually have an invitation to Caroline's wedding on Saturday, why don't I just stay that night, so I'm already there Sunday morning. I think I'll need a little adjustment time to get used to living amongst wolves before I travel with them," he said as doubts and concerns started to flood his brain, tempering his enthusiasm.

"Perfect. I better go now, love you, Tommy."

"Love you too, Tink. Night." He hung up the phone and let his head drop back on the headrest of his favorite chair.

He had just made the decision to quit his job, and take on not only a new job, but a whole new world. Talk about impulsive. It was unusual behavior for him, for sure, but this was an opportunity he didn't feel like he could pass up. This was the jump start he had been looking for, and he could feel it in his soul that it would be life altering.

Grabbing a beer on his way, he headed for his office to type up a letter of resignation and start packing for the trip. As he typed up his letter, he made a mental list of things to do before the weekend. Telling his parents was at the top of that list. He had always been close to his parents and Tina, so if he was going to leave the state it wasn't an option to leave them in the dark. Not to mention he needed someone to stop by the condo and pick up his mail while he was gone, and his mother had more time on her hands than Tina did.

Groaning at the thought of trying to explain this new job to his mother, he downed the rest of his beer. How was he going to avoid telling her more about Tina's new family, when he was about to become a part of it? He had been sworn to secrecy by Devin and Tina, and he had no intention of risking their lives by sharing their secrets with his gossipmonger mother.

A good night's rest was going to be necessary before the conversation, that was for sure, and it just so happened that he had to work the early shift tomorrow, so he didn't have time for a chat with the 'rents anyways. Other than them, he really had no one else to call. Not that he didn't have friends, but none that he was close enough to that they would be excessively concerned if they didn't hear from him for several weeks. His gym buddies were the only ones that would really miss him, and he could fill them in on his vacation and new job opportunity tomorrow.

Yes, tomorrow I'll deal with all of it, he thought to himself running his hand through his hair, *tonight I pack for a new adventure.* He started packing his bags for a trip that had no schedule or concrete plans and let himself bask in the excitement of the unknown. Even if he had some reservations about surrounding himself with wolves that were more powerful and dangerous than he was, he wasn't about to let this chance slip through his fingers.

Until recently, he had spent his life doing everything just right. He was a good kid that played sports all through high school. Basketball, baseball, and football took up all his free time, and ultimately baseball earned him a partial scholarship to college where he studied medicine. Taking the position at the wound care clinic seemed like a great thing when he finally graduated med school and was doggedly looking for a job. Many of his fellow classmates had gone on to work at major hospitals, but Thomas had resisted all the headhunters that contacted him. He had no idea at the time what the driving force behind his resistance was, but now he felt like this opportunity with the Gray Pack was what he had always been waiting for.

Other than his current addiction to boxing, he really had no hobbies. He spent a couple hours at the gym almost daily, sparring with the other gym rats that frequented Cabrioles. It was his way to let off steam, and keep his body fit and active, but it was also his way of avoiding turning into a hermit. He couldn't remember the last time he went on an actual date, although he had had no shortage of offers from the nurses at the clinic, and the gym bunnies that hung out near the boxing ring. There had just been no one recently that really got to him and attracted him on a physical and mental level. At this point it was likely that he would live a long healthy and single life.

C'est la vie, he thought to himself. *It's not like I have any great desire to be married and procreating.* His mother wouldn't be happy if he didn't settle down soon, but she would have to live with it. He was setting out on an adventure, and that's where his focus needed to be right now. Tomorrow he would think about his mother, tonight he would dream about werewolves.

Ring…Ring…Ring…

"Thomas! I'm so glad you called! I was just telling your dad that I hadn't talked to you in a few days."

"Hi, Mama. How are you both?"

"Good, good. Staying busy. Marjorie got me involved with a local quilting bee, and I've been practicing my machine quilting. I'm going to take a class on appliqué next month, and then I will be able to make a wedding quilt for your sister before her wedding."

"That's great, Mama. Listen, I called to let you know that I'm taking a vacation to Wyoming next week—"

"Wyoming? Why in the world would you go to Wyoming for a vacation?"

"I'm going to the mountains, Mom, taking a little time away from it all."

"And you're leaving next week?"

"Yeah, I'll leave on Sunday. A couple friends are going with me."

"On Sunday! How long have you had this planned?"

"It's kind of a spur-of-the-moment thing. Just some guys getting away to the wilderness for a little while."

"Thomas Josiah Jameson, don't you try to bluff your mother. After thirty-two years you would think that you would know better. Now, what is going on that you would take a vacation spur-of-the-moment like this?"

"Mama, I just needed some time away. I'm not sure I want to work at the clinic anymore, and I need to decide what my next step will be."

"And you're going to find the answers in Wyoming?"

"I hope so. Look, I just wanted to make sure that you and Dad knew where I was, and I wanted to ask you to keep an eye on my place for me while I'm gone."

"How long are you going to be wandering around in the mountains?"

"I'm not sure. I didn't set an end date just yet—"

"Oh my God! You're moving, aren't you? You're moving to *Wy-o-ming* and you're hiding it from me! Why would you want to move so far away, son? Is it your father and I? Are we too pushy? You know, I just want to be involved in your life somehow!"

"Mom! No! I'm not moving to Wyoming permanently, stop jumping the gun. I really truly am just taking a trip there, and when I get back I'll make more permanent decisions."

His mother was sniffling into the other end of the phone, and Thomas had to take several deep breaths to keep from snapping at her. As much as he adored his mother, he hated that she was so emotionally attached to him and Tina. *God help me if I ever find a wife, or in this case, God help her!*

"Will you keep an eye on my condo, Mama?"

"Of course, we will. You know I'm not trying to tell you how to live your life, but you really should think about dating…"

"I need to go, Mom. I just got paged by the nurse's desk. I'll try to call you later. Tell Dad I love him and give him a hug for me. I love you."

"Please take care of yourself, son. And I love you too, Thomas."

Clicking his cell phone off, Thomas dropped his head into his hands. Lying to his mom was tougher than he thought. All his life his parents had supported him in every endeavor. Standing on the sidelines through countless sporting events and helping him cover the cost of books or groceries when things got tight during medical school. They were the best parents he could have ever asked for, and yet, they barely knew him. As far as he knew they had no idea of the loneliness he felt inside and hid from the world.

It's not like he was suicidal, he was just disappointed with where his life had taken him so far. He always imagined that having a career as a successful doctor would actually fill a void in his heart, but it seemed to have made the emptiness even emptier. Maybe this trip would be the diversion he needed to get a handle on himself and start his new career with the Gray Pack on the right foot.

CHAPTER TWO

The following Monday morning...

Thomas paced the floor of his room in the Alpha's cabin, waiting for the sun to rise. On Saturday morning, he had arrived at the Gray Pack den for Caroline, Devin, and Damon's wedding. It was a beautiful ceremony, and he could see the love between the three of them like a glowing light coming off their skin. It made him wish for just a moment that he had someone to love, too. Caroline had looked radiant as she walked down the aisle and said her vows with the Gray twins. His favorite moment had been when she first stepped into view, and she saw the brothers for the first time. The look on her face was a priceless moment that squeezed Thomas's heart in his chest. Caroline had been like another sister to him for the last several years and seeing her find Nothappiness was more than he could have hoped.

Then yesterday Rafe and Ryley threw a surprise wedding for their mate, Shandi. The surprise affair delayed their leaving for Wyoming another day but seeing the joy on Shandi's face made it worth it, so

Thomas wasn't complaining. The biggest problem with all these happy couples surrounding him was just that it amplified his own loneliness. Sitting at the celebration dinner after the ceremony, he watched as most of the people he knew took to the dance floor holding their respective partners close and whispering words of love to them. Instead of joining into the party, he sat in a quiet corner, and just observed it with what he hoped was a blank expression on his face. He was happy for them all, and jealous of them at the same time.

Sunday night seemed to drag on forever as he waited in his room, pretending to read a book while everyone else slept, because his nerves were so jangled he couldn't think straight. When he slept he had dreams of wolves running, snarling, and snapping. They were chasing someone, but he couldn't see who, and he didn't think he was chasing the individual, too. For some reason he felt protective of whomever their quarry was. Each time he would wake up sweating and alert as if he were going to charge the pack of angry wolves. It didn't make any sense. The only explanation he could come up with was that he was antsy about being the only human, traveling into a pack of unknown wolves.

Devin assured him that he would be perfectly safe, but as with anything unknown there was a ripple of apprehension in his belly. Getting to know the guys that were traveling with them had been great. They had welcomed him into the fold after Tina had accepted her mating with Liam, so he felt comfortable with them for the most part. The only one he hadn't met yet was the elusive Katie Jo Whetstone, the sole reason for this mission.

According to Tina, she looked uncannily similar to her brothers, but Thomas had a difficult time seeing either of the two huge blond men as small, dainty women. He chuckled quietly. It wasn't like he wouldn't meet her. If they were driving all the way to Wyoming together he would have plenty of time to get to know all the werewolves going on the trip.

When the first rays of sunshine finally peeked over the top of the trees so he could see them, he sighed with relief, and slid his feet into his tennis shoes. He had to get out and run before he was cooped up in a car for twelve hours. Quietly leaving his room he made his way through the dark to the back door off the kitchen, when a voice startled him enough to make him jump.

"Where are you headed, Doc?"

He turned to find Cash standing next to the stove holding a cup of coffee. Cash Gray was a tall lean man that looked like he was born on a horse ranch in the middle of Texas. He usually wore a cowboy hat over his messy black hair and faded blue jeans over his boots. This morning he was without the boots, hat, and even a shirt. His curly black hair hung rumpled over his brow, and the lines of sleep were written under his eyes. His dark brown gaze was curious, but not accusing, so Thomas offered back a sheepish grin.

"I was going to take a quick run. I'm used to hitting the gym first thing in the morning, and I hate long car rides."

Cash laughed and set his coffee cup in the sink. "I was headed that way myself. If you don't mind me running in my fur, I'll join you."

"Really? You're going to shift and run?" Thomas was fascinated. The only other time he had seen someone shift, was when Cash was shot a couple months ago. Tina had just started dating Liam at the time, and when Cash was shot by a poacher in the woods, she suggested they bring him to Thomas for treatment to avoid questions. Thomas had managed to get the bullet out of the wounded man, only to watch in shocked awe as the man morphed into a wolf in front of his eyes.

After some explanation, now Thomas understood that werewolves could heal themselves from most injuries, but only if they were in their wolf form. If the bullet had remained in Cash's shoulder, he wouldn't have been able to heal himself because he was so weak from blood loss. Within minutes of having the bullet removed, Cash was on his feet and able to walk from Thomas's home. According to Tina, Cash was completely recovered within days. That was the day that Thomas learned that werewolves were a very real, but very secret part of society.

"It's not going to make you squeamish or anything is it? I mean, I have to be naked to shift…" Cash said, looking a little reluctant.

"I'm a doctor. I've seen plenty of naked people. Honestly, I just hope I don't weird you out by watching. I'm anxious to see someone shift when they're conscious," Thomas said, and then laughed with Cash as they headed out the back door into the yard.

Cash quickly stripped his jeans off, and standing naked in the morning dawn, his body shifted from a six-and-a-half-foot-tall giant man, to an enormous wolf. He rose at least four-foot-tall at the top of his head, and his fur was dark chocolate brown with streaks of black throughout. He waited silently for several moments while Thomas looked him over, and then he cocked his head in question.

"Can you shift back for a second?" Thomas asked, and before he could blink, Cash stood before him in human skin. "Whoa! Shit, man, does that hurt?"

Cash shrugged. "Not really. It did the first time I shifted when I was about twelve, but you get used to it. It can still be painful when I'm really worn out because I have less energy to put into the shift, but most of the time it's just as natural for me as sneezing. Now that you've had your time to gawk at my gorgeous body, can we get moving, Doc?"

Thomas laughed, as Cash shifted back, and they both set off at an even pace into the woods. Cash led Thomas down several foot trails, never getting so far ahead of him as to lose him. It was one of the best runs Thomas could remember. The forest surrounding the den was beautiful and teeming with small creatures. The smell of rain was on the air, but the sun brightened the trees as it rose slowly into the sky.

Several miles and nearly an hour later, Thomas followed Cash to a small cabin in a clearing. Immediately he knew that it was a special place. There was an aura of magic surrounding it. Flowers were planted next to the steps, and a very old rocking chair sat on the small front porch. He slowed his body until he was just jogging in place and looked questioningly at Cash. Shifting back into his human form, Cash gave him a grin.

"Sorry, I should have warned you I needed to make a quick stop. I wanted to say good-bye to Delaky and get her blessing before we leave."

"Who is Delaky?" Thomas asked, finally stopping his movements and following Cash up to the porch. It was awkward to be standing in the middle of the woods with a six-and-a-half-foot-tall naked man, on some stranger's porch. He was desperately trying not to think about his surroundings, so he could focus on Cash's response.

"Delaky is our pack shaman. You probably saw her at the weddings but weren't introduced. She is our healer, spiritual guide, elder, etcetera, basically our pack grandmother. I feel a very close connection to her, and I never leave the pack for an extended period of time without getting her blessing. It's bad juju," he answered with a chuckle.

"Bad juju? Really? I wouldn't have pegged you for a believer of magic or spirits or whatnot." Thomas stared at him in disbelief.

"I'm superstitious. No black cats, no breaking mirrors, salt over the shoulder if it spills, and I have a lucky belt buckle that I wear whenever I'm on stage. Without it, I can't sing a lick," he responded with a laugh, and his trademark grin. Thomas couldn't help but laugh with him as he waited while Cash knocked on the door of the cabin.

A very small woman answered the door with an intriguing smile. "You are slow in your good-byes this day, my child."

"I took the new doc on a quick run before I headed your way. You knew I wouldn't leave before I stopped to see you," Cash said, as he hugged her, and then stepped inside the cabin.

Thomas followed, and once in the door he was able to get a better look at Delaky. He was shocked to see that she wasn't at all the frail, elderly woman that he was expecting. Instead she was a stunning woman with long, white-blonde hair that hung nearly to her knees. She looked like an unpainted china doll, with blonde eyelashes and eyebrows, above her pale blue, nearly colorless eyes. She was such an unusual-looking woman, that it left him standing there gaping at her mutely. How had he not noticed her in the last couple days?

"Close your mouth healer, or a bug might be swallowed." She

cocked her head and looked him over. "Long ago you were expected. I am glad to meet you, healer."

"Healer? Well, I *am* a doctor, but please call me Thomas, ma'am." He stuttered, feeling awkward at having been caught gawking. He reached his hand out and jerked with a start when she cupped it in her tiny grip. Her palms were soft, but her skin was cold, as she turned his hand and looked at it as though reading a book.

"Intelligence and humility have mated into a human soul. Strength surrounds your heart. You will be a strong addition to the Gray Pack," she responded. Her eyes were twinkling, and he could have sworn he could see images flickering in their depths.

"Thank you, I appreciate having your support," he said fighting off a wave of discomfort, and trying to cover it with a smile.

"No thanks are necessary when truth is in my words. Young healer, you seek your passion, and find yourself unfulfilled. It will remain so until you accept your place in the cycle of nature. The life you have must be released, to embrace the fullness of your destiny," she said mysteriously. Thomas fumbled with how to respond to her. Was she crazy? When Cash didn't respond to his questioning glance he frowned down at the small woman. He didn't want to offend her or Cash, but she was clearly one nugget short of a Happy Meal.

"Delaky, are you saying that you can see Thomas's future?" Cash asked, excitement lighting up his eyes.

Delaky tilted her head in acknowledgement but didn't outwardly accept or deny his assumption. The whole thing was rather unusual to Thomas. Why would Cash believe anyone could see the future? What kind of culture did werewolves actually have?

"Well, thank you, I think. It's lovely to meet you, but Cash we should probably get back. We need to get going pretty early." He fidgeted, feeling like he was standing in the principal's office trying to get out of trouble. As her gaze searched his face, he found himself thinking that Delaky's eyes were old, even though she looked like a woman in her twenties. Any other time he would have thought that her agelessness was fascinating, but right now it was damn uncomfortable.

"The soul who is always in a rush will run from what he is meant to see. Now, child, have you bonded with your mate yet?" She took his other hand in hers and held them both in front of her, inspecting them. What could she possibly be seeing on his palms?

Thomas's blood was pulsing in his ears, and his stomach was jumping. He could feel some sort of electrical current on his skin wherever Delaky's fingers touched him. It took a moment for her words to register in his head. "Mate? Who, me?"

"Delaky, Doc is human, he doesn't have a mate," Cash said. His forehead was wrinkled with confusion, and he stared at Thomas and Delaky's joined hands just as intensely as she did.

"Pfft. Humanity does not release you from destiny. Our Alpha's mate is proof. Or have you forgotten the cubs she carries?" Delaky said, finally releasing Thomas's hand, and stepping over to the small stove. She poured tea from a steaming tea kettle into a small ceramic mug and took a sip as though she hadn't just made a declaration that shook Thomas's whole world to its core.

"Are you telling me that I have a mate amongst the Gray Pack wolves?" Thomas asked, his eyes darting to take in Cash's stunned expression.

"No. I see that you have not established the bonds yet. I will share no more. It is not for me to tell you what Fate has written," she said with a sigh. Offering them both a cup of tea, which they declined, she took a seat on a small, padded bench by the fireplace. Turning to Cash she spoke again. "Young Gray, you have a need for blessings upon your travels. Come to me."

Cash moved promptly to her side and placed his hand within hers. Thomas watched silently, as she ran her finger down Cash's palm just as she had done with his own, and then she lifted her eyes. "You will journey far, and there will be struggles on the path. It must be broken before all the pieces can be mended. You will have to betray to learn to follow."

Thomas ran his hand through his hair and huffed out a sigh of irritation. This woman spoke in riddles, and it was starting to get under his skin. He had no clue what she was talking about. Cash, however, seemed to take it in stride, and he bent and kissed the top of Delaky's head before turning back to Thomas.

"Ready to go?" he asked with a grin. His naked body was still completely relaxed, and Thomas wanted to scream in frustration as his own body vibrated with apprehension over Delaky's words.

"Seriously? That's it?" he snapped, and Cash shrugged. Delaky sipped at her tea and watched Thomas as he fought his own emotions. "Fine. Whatever. Let's go."

He stormed out of the house and down the path toward the tree line. He had no idea which direction the Alpha's cabin was, but he knew that Cash wouldn't let him wander off. This wasn't the way he had intended on starting his time with the Gray Pack. He didn't want to offend anyone, but that woman was clearly bat-shit crazy. There was no way that Cash would betray anyone, or that Thomas was going to be mated to a werewolf. He had already met the entire pack, and unless they had some females secreted away somewhere, there wasn't a chance he was attracted to any of the werewolves so far.

He heard Cash running up behind him on all four paws, and he slowed down. Turning his head, he met Cash's questioning dark brown eyes, and he shook his head. "I don't like all that mumbo jumbo hoodoo."

Cash's eyes darkened and he let out a growl. Clearly, he didn't appreciate Thomas's interpretation of the situation. "I'm sorry, man, I'm not trying to piss you off, but I don't believe in that stuff. Anyway, we need to get back to the cabin and help load up."

They took off again with Cash in the lead, and in a surprisingly short amount of time they were stepping from the trees into mass chaos. It was a startling change from the earlier solitude at dawn. Deciding now was not the time to pursue the discussion with Cash over Delaky's supposed prophecies of the future, he headed into the house, and straight up to his room. He couldn't worry about some crazy lady in the woods declaring his fate. He had too many other things to think about. Excitement tingled under his skin as he refocused on the coming adventure, and he found himself smiling as he stepped into the shower.

A half an hour later he emerged from his room with damp hair, and an excited tension humming through his body. Entering the kitchen, he found the pack Alphas, Devin and Damon, along with their pregnant mate, Caroline, sitting down to breakfast. Also, at the table were Jim and Sienna Gray, the former Alpha couple, and another couple who he knew to be Henley and Victoria Gray, Tina's soon to be in-laws.

"Morning, Doc," Devin said with a small wave, as he reached over and placed several pieces of bacon on Caroline's plate. She smacked his hand in admonishment, but she was grinning, and Devin winked back at her.

While her attention was on Devin, her other mate, Damon slipped an extra piece of ham onto her plate from her other side, and Thomas nearly laughed out loud. "Good morning, everyone. It smells fantastic in here."

"It should! The ladies have been cooking up a storm for almost an hour. Grab a seat and help yourself." Jim Gray might not be the Alpha of the pack anymore, but he still carried an air of authority that couldn't be denied.

Thomas followed his instructions and heaped his plate full of a variety of yummy looking foods. Settling into a seat at the end of the table, he paused and held his hand out to Henley Gray. "Hello, Mr. Gray, we haven't been introduced yet. I'm Tina's older brother, Thomas Jameson."

Henley took the hand, as his loud boisterous laugh filled the room. "Well, it's nice to meet you, son, but don't be calling me Mr. Gray again. I'm Henley, and this stunning woman is my wife, Victoria." Thomas smiled and shook Victoria's hand as well, and then turned to his plate.

"Thomas, I hear you're planning on staying with us for the long haul after the trip?" Victoria said, and he nodded.

"That's the plan. As long as you guys will have me, and I don't get myself killed on this trip."

Everyone laughed, but Devin spoke up. "Don't worry about that, Thomas. I'm sending you with six of our strongest wolves to help get the Quiver Creek Pack back here. Not to mention you will have KJ, who at least knows the area. I'm sure they can get you back here in one piece."

"Well that would certainly be my preference!"

Tina and Liam took that moment to enter the room, and Thomas stood up to give his little sister a hug. "Hey Tink, hi Liam."

"Tink?" Henley asked, looking between the two of them.

"Tinker Bell, actually," Thomas answered his question with a smile. "She was so small when she was little that she reminded me of a fairy, so I started calling her Tinker Bell. Tink came because she hated it so much."

Tina stuck her tongue out at him as everyone else laughed. "Yeah, yeah, yeah, laugh it up. There is nothing fairylike about me now."

Thomas assessed his sister for a moment, realizing how right she was. She stood five foot seven now, and though she was still very thin, she wasn't necessarily delicate. She had grown into a beautiful woman. Her brown almond-shaped eyes were identical to Thomas's own, but the rest of her features were feminine. She was a ballet dancer, so she moved with a fluid grace that most women envied, and her short black hair gave the illusion of an even longer line to her neck and back. She reminded him of a swan more than a fairy nowadays. Two years younger than Thomas, Tina had lived a lifetime more pain than he had, but he was happy to see her settled and planning a wedding with Liam.

The laughing group went back to breakfast, and Thomas found that he fit right into the fold. They were all very accepting and open with him, as though he was part of their family already. It was comforting and reassuring all at once. They began to scatter as they finished eating, some headed to work on last minute arrangements for the trip, while others had to go to work. Thomas watched as Tina kissed Liam good-bye, before she came around the table to hug him too. He wrapped his arms around her slim frame and breathed in her apple-cinnamon scent.

"Stay safe, Tommy. I need you back here to help me set up the clinic," she said with a grin.

"I'll be back before you know it, Tink. Love you."

"Love you, too." With that she waved good-bye, and Thomas watched Liam's face change in a second. His open, laughing smile closed up, and he looked slightly lost.

"You all right, Liam?"

"Yeah, I'll be fine," Liam said with a heavy sigh. He turned to face Thomas, his eyebrow ring winking in the sunlight from the window. For the umpteenth time Thomas wondered how this playboy managed to convince his baby sister to settle down with him.

The story Tina had told him was that she and Liam stumbled into each other when Tina was kidnapped along with Caroline. The kidnapper was the Diego Pack Alpha, Barton Diego, and he was intent on raping and murdering them both. Once the two women were rescued, Liam had his hands full convincing Tina to even give him a chance. It wasn't that she didn't have feelings for him, but Tina went through a painful period of grief and guilt when her fiancé was killed five years earlier in a mugging. Actually, it sounded like Liam and Tina connected via their grief once Liam shared his own tragic history. Liam's daughter Daphne and his ex-wife Roxy had been killed in a car wreck just a couple years back.

Outside of his parents, Thomas had never seen two souls better suited to each other. Except perhaps Caroline, Devin, and Damon, but *that* was three souls, and they were a predestined match. Remembering the activities of the day before, Thomas had to admit that Rafe, Ryley, and Shandi seemed to share the same connection, and jealousy didn't sit well in his belly. Someday, he told himself. He would find a woman that completed him like that, someday.

Making his way into the living room, he was hit with the overwhelming scent of rain and fresh air. A quick glance out the front wall of windows assured him that the sun was still shining brilliantly in the sky where it had been an hour ago, but now a woman stood in the middle of the living room, her compact, sexy little body had his cock thickening in his pants before he could even second-guess his reaction to her. Lifting his eyes, his gaze zeroed in on a pair of gorgeous blue eyes staring back at him from a dainty, heart-shaped face, surrounded by a cloud of blonde hair. Lust hit him full force, and he inhaled sharply. Her face flushed a pretty pink color, just before she ran from the room without a word.

It was another moment before he could breathe again, and he glanced around him to see Damon standing in the doorway apparently watching the escaping woman run in the other direction. Thankfully, he didn't seem to notice Thomas's reaction to her. Mentally shaken, Thomas grasped for a logical explanation for his irrational physical reaction to the stranger. He considered going after her but decided that it probably wasn't a good idea in his current state. His heart was racing, and his cock was pounding so hard against his zipper that he was surprised it held.

"Who was that?" he asked Damon, as he turned around and came in the house.

"Oh, that was KJ, didn't she introduce herself?" Damon asked in confusion.

"No, but she seemed to be in a hurry," Thomas said, trying to gather his thoughts, and control his libido.

"Huh, well, she does seem to be an unusual girl. You'll get to know her well on the trip, I'm sure. Hopefully she's not this rude all the time," Damon said with a chuckle as he headed up the stairs, leaving Thomas alone again in the living room.

It took him a moment to process that this was the infamous sister of Rafe and Ryley, and the driving force behind this road trip to Wyoming. Come to think of it, there was a slight resemblance there, but thankfully she was a beautiful version of the two Nordic looking giants. So why did she run away from him like he was a Roman invader coming to pillage and plunder? A haze covered his vision at the mental image of pillaging and plundering the sweet little blonde armful. That wasn't going to happen, but it was a nice fantasy.

Maybe she was just shy, or uncomfortable around strangers. He knew his eyes weren't betraying him, he had seen desire in her gaze, right before the panic set in and she took off.

"Thomas?" a voice behind him drew him from his musings, and he turned to face Caroline. She was his little sister's best friend and had become an important part of his family. He would protect her just like he would Tina, and he was glad to see her happily married to the twins. The current frown on her face told him that he wasn't hiding his thoughts very well. "Are you okay, Tommy? You look a little flushed."

He tried to give her a smile of reassurance, but he knew it probably looked more like a grimace. "I'm great, but I appreciate your concern. I suppose I'm just a little restless. Nervous energy and all that. Do you know how much longer it will be before we get on the road?"

Caroline gave him a quick hug before she plopped down on the overstuffed sofa and rubbed her burgeoning belly. Pregnant with twins, her belly was rounding out quickly, and she glowed with happiness. "Damon said everything should be ready in the next half an hour. By the way, thank you for doing this. We really appreciate it."

"No problem, I was getting restless at the wound care clinic, and considering leaving anyway. You guys just gave me a good reason. Can I ask you a couple questions?" He moved to sit in a chair across from her.

"Sure, what's up?"

"How does the pack hierarchy work? I mean, are you the queen? Are Devin and Damon supposed to be joint kings? I want to understand, so I don't put my foot in my mouth at some point."

"Kind of. See in a wolf pack there is always an Alpha male, and an Alpha female. In our particular case Devin is the Alpha, and I'm the Alpha Bitch—although I hate that particular title, so Her Majesty works just as well," she said with a wink and a laugh. "Damon is technically a Beta wolf, but because they are twins, everyone calls them the Alphas of the pack. He is Devin's second, his vice president so to speak. After the Alphas are the Betas, they are the strongest men in the pack. They tend to handle security, and any pack business that comes along. Kind of like our own Security Council, it's actually a coveted position. Then the next level are the Omegas, they are usually made up of males, and occasionally females, like Tina and Tawny, who have proven their strength. It's not that they are less worthy than the Betas, but they are mostly the fastest, sneakiest, and the brainiest. They are the go-to people for spying if we're in a situation to need it, or for taking care of the pack while the Betas are occupied. In Tawny's case she is one hell of a computer hacker, so she made Omega because the pack needs her skills occasionally. The last level, and the one that most wolves fall into, are the Deltas. Does that help?"

"Yes, actually it does. Where does Delaky fit into that?"

She looked surprised. "Delaky? Oh, well, she's a special case altogether. The way I understand it, everyone alive today remembers her being here and looking the exact same as she does today. She never ages, she never changes. She just is."

"So she is immortal?" he asked, and he cringed because he could hear the doubt in his own voice.

"You might say that, but I honestly don't know. Delaky speaks in riddles, I'm sure you caught on if you've met her, so we can't always grasp the message she's trying to relay. She seems to see into the future and the past easily, but she doesn't just walk up to random people spouting off prophecies. Usually she will wait until she's asked. She has some skill in healing, but she seems happy to be relieved of that duty with you coming on board."

"I'm glad to hear that, and yes, I did notice the puzzle speak when I met her. Cash took me to her cabin this morning when we went on a quick run. She seems to believe that I will be meeting my own mate shortly," Thomas said running his hand through his hair.

"What?" Her gasp startled him, and he stared across the room into her shocked face. "Are you telling me that she thinks you have a mate within the pack?"

"No, she never said that specifically, she just asked me if I had bonded with my mate yet, and when I questioned her, she said that I hadn't established a bond yet, and it was not for her to tell me what Fate has written. Crazy, huh?"

Caroline practically leapt from the couch and across the room. Grabbing his hands in hers, she pulled him up from his seat into a hug. "That's fantastic, Thomas! You're going to be part of the family for real now! I wonder who it is? I would have figured you had met everyone in the pack already and felt the mating lust, but if Delaky says she's here, then she must be!"

Thomas rested both hands on the petite woman's shoulders trying to hold her still and calm her enthusiasm. "Whoa, Caro, slow down. I'm not sure I believe anything she said, but I can promise you that I already consider myself part of the pack family."

"Oh, but if you have a werewolf mate, then she would turn you after you bonded, and believe me, the mating lust is unavoidable. It hit me square in the gut." She paused and glanced down at her rounded belly, giggling. "Obviously."

"We'll see, Caro. For now, I have a mission to accomplish before I can worry about my future," he said with a grin. Caroline was so full of sparkle now that she had met the Gray twins. There was a time when he worried that she would cut herself off from the world instead of facing it head on, but she seemed to have overcome her grief for her parents. They were killed in the World Trade Center, and it wasn't long after that, that Tina and Caroline met in nursing school. When Tina first introduced him to Caroline, she was a sad, withdrawn woman who held herself with very little confidence. Now she sparkled from the inside out.

"Yes, you do! I'm just praying that you guys can get there in time. The way KJ talked about her mom's injury…It sounds like she might already be septic. Silver can be lethal for werewolves, and Devin is afraid that the bullet in her arm is silver so she's slowly being poisoned to death," Caroline said. Her face grew slightly pale, and she rubbed at her belly nervously.

"I'll do everything I can to help her, Caro. I'm no expert in werewolves, but I'll do my best."

"I know that, Tommy. I hate that the pack has to be split like this, but with the Diego wolves coming our way shortly, we just have to divide and conquer." She stepped away from him and pressed the palm of her hand to her forehead. "Hmm. The babies need to eat again, they always get restless when they are hungry."

"Didn't you just eat? You can feel them already? Aren't you only a couple months along?" he asked.

"Almost four months, but I've been feeling them for several weeks. According to the twins' mom, Sienna, the gestation period for werewolves is much shorter than humans. Only about six months. It makes it more difficult for us to blend into human careers, but with me quitting my job to spend more time here at the den it's not a problem for me," Caroline said, leading the way into the kitchen.

"Six months, holy shit! You're almost to the end already!" Thomas said stumbling a little as he followed her. "Caro, I'm not sure I'm comfortable delivering your babies. With the birth of multiples there can be all kinds of complications, and with you being a werewolf there are added hurdles that I haven't even learned about yet."

Pulling a tray full of sliced ham out of the refrigerator, she laughed. "It's okay, Tommy, I understand. Delaky will deliver the twins for me because she has delivered every baby brought into the pack for more decades than we can even comprehend. I would prefer she continue to deliver babies, if you don't mind."

Thomas gave an exaggerated sigh of relief. "Thank God! O.B. has never been my preferred field. I'll stick with doctoring up the injured and sick, and I am happy to let her handle the female issues."

She laughed with him as she snacked on the ham. The sound of the front door banging open was followed by the enticing scent of the mysterious KJ from earlier. Thomas felt his body respond immediately, and he turned toward the living room.

"Excuse me for a minute, Caro," he said, and he followed the sweet smell without waiting for Caroline's response.

She was standing next to the stairs, with just a pair of blue jeans snuggly covering her lush ass. Petite perfection, her body was curved in all the right places, and he clenched his fists at the urge to hold it against his own. The skin of her naked back looked softer than a rose petal, and he felt a twinge of regret as she tugged a shirt over her head, and turned around.

Her eyes were closed, and her face grew very pale, turning a scary gray color. Hurrying across the room, he gripped her shoulders, worry snaking through his belly. "Are you all right, little one?"

He inhaled sharply as her eyes popped open, staring up into his face with white hot lust in them. Her lips were parted slightly, and her tongue darted out to wet them, making him rock hard in a second. Pulling his hands away from her to keep from pushing her up against the wall and ravishing her, he cleared his throat, and pushed his hands into his pockets. "Are you all right? You looked like you were going to pass out."

Her soft growl had him stepping backward, but she seemed to sway with his movement, and he caught her up against him, refusing to let her fall. Fear overrode his desire as he imagined all sorts of health problems that would cause her to faint. "It's okay KJ, I've got you. Come on. Let's get you laid down for a minute. When did you eat last? Are you ill?"

She let him lead her to the couch, where he sat her down, and then crouched in front of her. He had to adjust his position to keep from cutting the circulation off to his cock, as his body reacted to her closeness. He ran his hand down her arm to take her pulse, jumping a little when she jerked it from his grip violently and pushed him away from her.

"Stop! Stop it! I'm fine!" she snarled at him, and he sat back on his heels in shock.

"You nearly fainted. I don't call that fine," he responded as he looked her over. Her sunshine-colored hair was long and fell in wild curls down her back. Her blue eyes were the color of the sky, but if he wasn't mistaken there was a tiny ring of green surrounding her dilated pupils.

"I just got a little lightheaded, that's all. I'm fine. How did you know my name?" she asked with a frown.

"I've met everyone else in the pack. You and I are the only strangers around here right now, so the process of elimination made it pretty simple. I'm Thomas Jameson," he said, holding his hand out to her in introduction. She hesitated, staring down at his extended hand like it was a snake about to bite. He watched in fascination as she swallowed hard and took a deep breath before gripping his hand. Electricity shot through his arm into his brain, and he gasped at the same time as she growled.

"Oh shit," she whispered while he just sat there staring at their joined hands in shock.

"Hey guys! I see you've finally met each other. Are you two about ready to leave? Noah and Luke have almost all the bags loaded." Owen stepped into the room, looking anxious, but the moment his eyes landed on them, Thomas could see his nostrils flare, and his gaze harden. Sunlight flashed off the diamond earring in his earlobe, as he jerked his head to run his gaze over KJ before glaring at Thomas. "KJ, are you all right?"

She nodded silently, and Thomas glanced from her to Owen waiting for an explanation. It was obvious that Owen sensed the tension between them, but there was something else there. Thomas forced himself to release her hand and stand up.

"I still have my bag in here," KJ said, seeming to gain control over her reaction quicker than he could. "I'll run it out to the van."

"Just give it to me, KJ, I'll take it out there," Owen said, as KJ moved to pick up the duffel bag by the stairs. Thomas bit the inside of his cheek to hold back a groan as her nipples poked through the thin fabric of her T-shirt. His mouth watered, and his brain was slightly fuzzy. It was almost like he was a sixteen-year-old virgin again.

Owen stepped over and relieved her of the bag against her protest, and then he turned to Thomas and cocked his head, staring hard at him. "Doc, why don't you come on out to the van with me?"

Thomas hesitated. He wanted to question KJ about what had just transpired, and the electrical response between their bodies, but the pale color of her cheeks, and the fear in her blue eyes stopped his voice in his throat. She was scared of him, or of the situation. There was definite fear in the air. With another deep breath, he nodded at Owen, and said softly, "Nice to meet you, KJ, maybe we can talk on the trip."

She nodded, but didn't speak, and Owen's narrowed gaze ran over the two of them again, before he gestured for Thomas to lead the way outside. *Well that was a memorable introduction. What am I supposed to take from all that,* he thought as he moved out into the bright sunshine? Oddly, his body seemed to resist leaving KJ behind in the house, and his stomach rolled a little bit. Forcing his lips to return the smiles of the waiting men outside, he headed toward the two large vans packed with their gear, Owen at his side. He would get his answers at a more opportune time, no doubt about it.

CHAPTER THREE

KJ rested her forehead against the glass window as she stared out at the passing scenery. To her right, Cash dozed with his long legs stretched out as far as the cramped van would allow. In the front seat, Ryley and Noah chatted about various subjects ranging from fishing to firefighting. The other four people on the trip, Rafe, Owen, Luke, and Thomas were in the van behind them as they coasted down I-70 through Kansas.

They were heading back to Wyoming, where she had left behind her parents, friends, and everything she had ever known to make the journey to the Gray Pack den. It took her three weeks in wolf form to travel the distance, and there had been Kaplan Pack trackers on her heels the whole way. She kept having to double back to lose them when they were getting too close to her. It was a life or death mission, and the relief she felt when she woke up to find herself in Devin Gray's cabin was only temporary. There was still a long road in front of her to get back to her parents and see them safely transported to Kansas City.

The Kaplan wolves hadn't gotten close enough to attack her until she finally reached Gray Pack territory, but the wolf that did caught her completely unaware. The only thing that she remembered about the attack was seeing a dusty, brown wolf flying at her through the bushes, and screaming out in pain as his canines sunk into the flesh of her leg. She lost consciousness from that point on, but the story she got from Caroline was that her brothers and their adopted father were the ones to find her in the woods and get her safely transported to the Alpha's cabin.

It was surreal now, seeing Rafe and Ryley, because they both looked so much like her father. There was a clear resemblance to herself and her mother too, so she couldn't deny that there was shared blood between them all. For the last twenty-four years she had listened to her parents talk about returning to reclaim their sons. She had heard them go on and on about how great the Gray Pack was compared to everyone else. Never had she disagreed, argued, or even voiced her opinion until they asked her to go by herself to find her brothers and get help.

Logically, she knew that her mother was dying of her injury. There had been clear evidence of her decline before KJ left three weeks ago, but her heart hoped for a miracle. She could only pray that they could make it back in time with Thomas to save her life. Thomas. The sexy human doctor, who made her wolf howl. Her mate. What the hell was fate thinking pairing *her* with a human? It felt like some sort of sick joke. She was standing on the edge of her future, ready to bolt and embrace a whole new world, only to be stopped by something so restricting as a mate. She let out a huff of irritation that drew Cash's attention from his half-asleep state.

"What's up, sweetheart? You look like you lost your best friend," he said quietly, so as not to interrupt the other two in the front seat.

"No, I'm just thinking. I'm worried about my mom. She wasn't doing very well when I left, and that was three weeks ago."

Cash nodded. "Yeah, I can see why that would upset you, but we have Doc with us, and if anyone can help it's him. He saved my life after all. Tell me about your pack mates. You said that everyone was outcasts or rogues? How did they end up all lumped together?"

KJ shifted so she could face Cash. "I was wondering when

someone would start asking for details other than how many of us there were. When I was little it was just Mom, Dad, and me, but they ran into Rudy while I was still a baby. He was a rogue that had been on his own for years, but as he aged, he was having more trouble staying off the grid. He's ancient, or at least he looks it to me. I asked him once how old he was, and he just laughed and told me, 'Old enough.'"

Cash chuckled. "Well that's a loaded gun."

"Yeah, but that's Rudy. Anyway, he helped teach Mom and Dad more about how to hide their scent, and how to avoid detection, so the Omegas from the Kaplan Pack couldn't keep following them. They were always on their guard, one step ahead of a pack of bloodthirsty wolves with orders to bring only Tasha Whetstone back to Alaska alive."

"Wow. I can't imagine what that was like for them with a small baby to protect," Cash said, shaking his head. The silence in the van was overwhelming, and KJ glanced up to see Ryley watching her in the rearview mirror as he drove, and Noah turned around to face her so he could listen.

"I'm sure it was difficult, but I was too young to know it. As I grew up Mom and Dad constantly reminded me of the need to stay close and protect myself. I remember nights when Mom would wake me up and we would run as fast and as far as our paws could take us, leaving everything we had behind. We would start over in some new strange place, stealing and begging to put food in our bellies. I was six I think, when Louisa and Orlando joined us. They were outcasts from a pack in Mexico. I'll let them tell you their story because it's a painful one. They were on the run, too, and we were more than willing to accept them into our family in exchange for their strength in hunting, scavenging, and the added eyes and ears. Next to join the fray were Brick and Kelly Poplin. They are mated, but they were rogues that somehow managed to find each other. They have two kids now, little boys who are cute as hell, Axel and Jordan."

"Kelly was a female rogue?" Ryley asked in surprise, and she nodded.

"There are more than you might think out there. She said that she left her pack when her father tried to force her into a mating with a wolf that wasn't her true mate. Anyway, after the Poplins joined us we stumbled over the small canyon that Quiver Creek runs through. It was the perfect place for us to set up camp, but we never expected to live there for so long. The Kaplan Omegas either lost track of us for the next fifteen years or they gave up the hunt for a while. Either way, they backed off, and we had fifteen years of a fragile peace. The Griffin family, the Todd family, and several male rogues all came during that time frame. In total there were twenty-two of us when I left three weeks ago, but the Kaplan wolves had been prowling closer and becoming more dangerous over the last several months. They were shooting at our security patrols, and doing things like poisoning our water supply, so I don't know who is left."

"Don't worry. We'll get everyone back to the den, and then we'll figure out what to do to deal with Nicolas Kaplan. That man can't be allowed to continue raising hell like this," Cash said, patting her knee in reassurance.

"Thank you, but you can't promise me that we will get everyone back to Kansas City safely. Not after I've seen the Kaplan wolves shooting at the women and children of our pack just for fun. They seem to have no qualms about hurting someone," she said, gritting her teeth in anger.

"Well they haven't met the Gray Pack yet. It's about time they came face-to-face with someone their own size," Ryley said, winking at her in the mirror, while Cash and Noah cheered, and exchanged fist bumps.

"Are all packs so close to each other?" she asked out of pure curiosity. It seemed like these men were all brothers instead of just pack mates.

Cash shrugged. "I don't really know. We don't travel between packs very often. Our most recent dealing with another pack was the Diegos. Their den is up by Chicago, and their pack Alpha had a mean streak in him. He also had a grudge against Devin, so he challenged Dev to an Alpha battle."

KJ gasped. "A battle for dominance?"

Noah snorted. "Yeah, but before they even had a chance to fight, Barton Diego showed his true colors. Like the chickenshit that he was, he kidnapped two of our women, Caroline and Tina. He was going to rape and kill them, just to get under Devin's skin. Man, he never knew what hit him when Caroline shifted into her wolf for the first time during the attack, and then the rest of the Gray Pack Betas crashed into the house. I sure as hell wish I could have been there."

"Oh my God. Were Caroline and Tina okay?" she asked, leaning forward as she became engrossed in the story.

"Oh yeah, they were a little beat up and scared, but they were fine. That's when Liam realized that Tina was his mate. Damn, that girl gave him a run for his money," Ryley answered. "She didn't want any part of mating into a werewolf pack."

"Really? So she turned him down?" KJ asked.

"Oh yeah, in a big way. He had to put major effort into winning her over. Of course, it didn't help when one of her coworkers started poaching wolves on pack land, and tried to poach Tina," Noah said with a loud laugh.

"Poach her? You mean he tried to kill her? That poor woman!" KJ gasped.

Cash held up a hand. "Not exactly, see Carter Lawrence was trying to take her home with him. He found her out at the lake when he was out there hunting wolves and decided to drag her home with him against her will. She got stuck...umm..." Ryley and Noah started laughing harder from the front seat.

"What? What am I missing?" KJ asked growling in irritation.

"She got stuck in a tree! It's not nearly as funny if you weren't there, but trust me, Cash and I had to go with Liam to rescue her. She was stuck in a tree because her boobs were too big to fit through the space between branches. It gave us just enough time to rescue her,"

Ryley explained, trying to keep it together as laughter threatened to consume him.

KJ couldn't stop the grin from spreading over her face as she pictured the slim woman with large breasts and how she must have looked stuck in a tree. "So what happened to the guy?"

"His attorney pled insanity on his behalf, so he's in a hospital getting treatment. Tina is no worse for the wear, although I pity the next man that thinks he can kidnap that she-wolf. She has Alpha Bitch tendencies and a sore spot for kidnappers," Cash said, wiping tears from his cheeks as he laughed.

"Good grief. Your women seem to be a lot of trouble," KJ said with a shake of her head.

"Nah, not all of them. Shandi wasn't any trouble for Rafe and I. All I had to do was turn on my charm," Ryley said smugly.

"Oh yeah, I've seen that legendary charm. Didn't she go running out of a bar trying to escape your *charm?*" Cash said, smacking Ryley upside the back of his head.

They all laughed harder when Ryley growled and then groaned with a nod of his head in admission. KJ couldn't believe she was actually enjoying herself. These guys were turning out to be easier to get along with than she first expected. She knew that Rafe still wasn't ready to be friends yet, but truth be told she wasn't sure she even liked her oldest brother. He seemed so gruff and serious. Shandi was kind-hearted, and her nature was truly generous. KJ had only one female friend even close to her age. Lily Griffin was twenty-six, and other than her the only people close to KJ in age were male and had no friendly interest in her. After the time one of them tried to make a move on her, and she nearly ripped his arm from his body to escape, none of them ever attempted to touch her again.

Until today, there hadn't been any males of any species that she was even remotely attracted to. To her, being mated was akin to being chained with silver to the stove, and forced to cook, clean, and breed babies. It wasn't the life she wanted for herself.

Even the distant thought of Thomas Jameson in the other van

filled her stomach with butterflies, and made her palms sweat. Her fingers itched to run through his dark brown hair, while she got lost in his almond-shaped brown eyes. What would his mustache and goatee feel like against her skin, for that matter, what would his lips feel like on hers? She closed her eyes and rested her head against the seat, trying to think about anything else but him.

A silent tension filled the van, and she cracked her eyes to find Noah and Cash both gaping at her with wide eyes. "What?" she snapped.

The two men exchanged looks, and she glanced up to see Ryley glaring at Cash in the rearview mirror. "What the fuck, man? That's my sister." He growled at Cash, who threw his hands up.

"Not me, dude! I don't know what has her all worked up," Cash said shifting in his seat. KJ frowned at Noah who was still staring at her, his nostrils flaring. She took in a deep breath, catching the musky scent of desire, and she groaned loudly. They could smell her desire, and they thought it was because of one of them.

"Shit. No! It's not either of them, Ryley. I don't want either one of them, I promise!" she said, trying to calm her racing heart, and her jumpy hormones.

"Thank God!" Ryley sighed.

"Hey!" Cash protested.

"Why not, sugar? I promise I'll make it good for you," Noah said with a wink as he blew her a kiss. Ryley reached out and smacked him, before he turned his attention back to her.

"KJ, who is it? Don't try to deny it. I'm a mated wolf, I know the scent of the mating lust," Ryley said. His hands were clenched around the steering wheel so tightly that his knuckles were white.

"No one. It's no one." She lied, turning her head to the windows. "Besides, he's not for me."

"Not for you? Are you mad? Well if you're not now, you will be when you deny your wolf her mate." Ryley's voice was tight with frustration, and Cash and Noah looked decidedly uncomfortable. "Believe me when I tell you that you can't ignore what you're feeling. I went through it with Shandi. I don't know how I ever thought I could walk away from her, but I did at one point."

"This is none of your business, Ryley. We may be family by blood, but you haven't earned the right to pull the big brother act on me yet. Back off." She could feel her wolf rising to the surface with her anxious energy.

"Not my business, are you kidding me?" Ryley yelled. The van swerved slightly, and then he pulled off the highway into a rest stop lane. Without saying anything else, he parked the van, and got out, slamming the door behind him.

She cursed beneath her breath as Cash and Noah exited the van. To her surprise they turned around, expectantly waiting for her to follow. When she shook her head sitting still in her seat, Cash growled at her. "Don't be ridiculous. You may as well get out of the car and stretch your legs. We have a long drive still ahead of us, and who knows when Pissy-Pants will want to stop again."

She gave a loud huff and started to crawl across the seat to climb out, when Thomas's scent hit her nose. She gasped, and tumbled out of the van, cringing as Cash and Noah both rushed to help catch her. So much for being graceful amongst strangers, she thought to herself. A third male body stood nearby, and without looking she knew it was Thomas.

Mate.

Her wolf clearly had no problem accepting its fate. She took a deep breath and stood, nodding to the guys that she was fine, but Cash didn't release her elbow right away. Looked up at him in confusion, she was even more stunned to see his hard glare, as he looked between her and Thomas. Cash's nostrils flared, and she felt the rush of blood fill her cheeks, knowing that he was scenting her desire. Embarrassed and ashamed of herself she jerked her arm away from him.

Without lifting her head, she muttered, "Thank you, Cash," and wrapped her arms protectively around her waist. With a toss of her blonde hair she glanced back toward where Rafe and Ryley were arguing. They were too quiet for even her wolf ears to hear, but she knew they were both upset. Their muscular bodies were tight with tension, and they both kept glancing her way.

Thomas seemed to be drawn toward her like they were two magnetic matches, and she felt him move closer. Within touching distance, he stopped. "KJ? Can I talk to you for a minute?"

Clenching her jaw tightly together, she tried to inhale through her mouth instead of her nose. Instead of giving her relief it made her think about what he would taste like. Her mouth watered at the thought, and she bit her own lip to keep a moan from slipping out.

Her eyes darted around her, looking for an escape. It seemed that everyone else had disappeared all of a sudden. She was left standing alone with Thomas, only her brothers in sight. His large body seemed to overwhelm hers and she felt tiny standing next to him. She was trembling as she tried to gain control of the wolf inside of her, and she opened her mouth to decline, only to hear her own voice saying, "Okay."

Thomas reached out and took her hand, pulling it away from her body and lacing his fingers through hers. She could have sworn she heard a crackle of electricity as their skin touched again. Thomas led her away from the vans and down a short footpath off the side of the rest stop parking lot. It meandered about forty feet into a small park that was encircled by trees. There was another couple a little way away, but they were walking away down the path.

The moment that they were out of view from everyone, Thomas spun around to face her. The blazing heat in his brown eyes rocked her to the core, and she fell against his chest. The heat from his body against hers brought a soft sigh of contentment from her lips. He felt so perfect, and she fit so nicely into his arms. This is what it meant to be held by your mate. She wanted desperately to resist it, but all she could do was melt into him.

She lifted her face up to look at him, unsure of what to expect. If he felt half of the turbulence that she did right now, she didn't think they would survive the mating lust. His chocolate eyes were nearly black with confusion and lust, and his jaw was clenched tight.

"Little one, I'm not exactly sure what's happening here, but I hope you feel it too." The rumble of his lust-tightened voice made her belly quiver and her pussy muscles clench.

"I feel it, too. Damn it." Her snarl was met with his tight groan of need, just before he captured her mouth. Fire raced through her blood from the top of her head to the soles of her feet and she arched into him. The friction of his chest against hers was mind-numbing.

His hands slid down to cup her ass and lift her higher against his body. Instinctively she locked her ankles behind his butt, her thighs riding tightly around his lean hips. The hard ridge of his erection pressed against the seam of her jeans giving her the pressure she craved against her swollen clit. She rocked against him, tilting her hips forward to provide the perfect cavity for his cock to nestle, and he cursed against her mouth.

Biting her bottom lip, he dug the fingers of one hand into her ass, and his other hand snaked up to cup her breast. A sharp pinch on her nipple made her gasp and cream in her panties, and she broke the kiss to throw her head back and press her breast further into his massaging palm.

"God, you're beautiful, KJ." He cupped her aching tit in his large hand and tweaked the nipple with his thumb. Even through her bra and shirt, his fingertip was heaven against the sensitive bud, making her moan. Suddenly, he was releasing her, and dropping her back to the ground. His hands were threading into her hair and holding her in place while he rested his forehead against hers. "Damn it all to hell. I want to just take you here and now, little one, but I'm afraid your brothers would rip my throat out and bury my body."

She couldn't stop the laughter that bubbled from her throat, "You're right, Doc. Even though they don't know me, they don't seem to want anyone fucking with me."

"Baby, I damn sure plan on fucking with you, but I will wait until we have more privacy."

The grin that spread over his face made her cunt pulse, and she felt her own stickiness dripping down her thighs. She glanced behind him into the park, but there was no one else around now, and she sighed with relief just before a masculine growl sounded from behind her.

Spinning, she came face-to-face with Luke and Noah. The first man looked pissed off, while the second wore an arrogant grin and winked back at her like they hadn't just seen her climbing up Thomas Jameson's long, hot body.

"Well, well, well, so I see the Doc didn't waste any time, huh?" Noah said with a wiggle of his eyebrows.

"What the hell are you doing?" Luke snarled; his cheeks red with rage. His eyes glowed, and if she wasn't mistaken, she thought she could see the hint of claws starting to protrude from his fingertips.

"None of your fucking business, Luke!" she snapped back, bracing herself in case he came at her.

"Easy now, little one, he's just being protective," Thomas said against her ear, and his arms came around her waist to lay flat on her abdomen.

"No, he's just being a moron. I don't believe either one of us invited you to this private moment, Luke, so turn around and go back to the vans." She shrugged out of Thomas's grip, feeling less confident about the situation than she had just moments ago. This wasn't what she wanted, was it? She didn't want or need a mate in her life, but she had very nearly claimed one, in every way possible. "Actually, never mind, you three stay here and fight it out, I'm going back to the van. We don't have time for this shit."

She stormed away from Thomas, pushing between Noah and Luke who didn't fight her as she moved past. Good choice, she thought to herself. Her anger was running high and her control was thin. If one of them tried to stop her now, she was likely to shift and teach him a lesson about invasion of privacy.

Making her way back to the van, she inhaled a deep breath only to curse sharply at her own scent. Fuck a duck, there were some days where being a wolf just didn't pay off. Her wolf was whining in her head, desperate to get back to its mate and finish what they started. And knowing that every man she was traveling with, save one, would know the direction of her thoughts just pissed her off even more.

Rafe stepped out from behind the van just as she tugged the door open. "Don't start the big brother routine—"

His growl startled her, cutting off her words. "I'm not starting anything and neither are you. I get it, you want the Doc, but this is serious, KJ. He's not a werewolf, he's human, which means that he doesn't understand what's happening to him."

"What exactly do you think is happening to him, Rafe?" she snapped back.

"The mating lust." His blue eyes dared her to deny it, and she flushed under his scrutiny.

"You don't know what you're talking about. Just because I'm attracted to him—"

He threw his head back and laughed arrogantly. "Attracted to him? Honey, I could smell your desire a mile away. I just went through it, KJ. If anyone gets it, it's me. You need to tell him. He deserves to know and understand what's to come."

He stood there silently glaring at her, and she fidgeted uncomfortably. Why did he have to say anything? Why couldn't he just pretend he didn't know what was going on, and leave her the hell alone?

"You know, I don't appreciate you deciding that you're going to take on the role of my caretaker, when you don't even fucking like me," she said petulantly, crossing her arms over her aching breasts, and leaning against the side of the van.

"I don't know you, so I can't say whether or not I like you." While she appreciated his honesty, his words stabbed into her gut, reminding her of the crazy mission they were on. "I would do the same thing for any female wolf under my protection, and make no mistake, right now you *are* under my protection. My Alpha put you there, and apparently, so did your parents."

"They are *your* parents too, dumbass," she muttered under her breath. Her rage had settled, and so had her lust. Now she just felt a sense of lonely emptiness.

"I believe that you believe that, but I need more than just your word. Now, I'm going to give you a little time to get things right in your head, but you need to realize that you can't stop the mating lust once it's started. It will overwhelm you if you try to fight it, and eventually it will drive your wolf mad. That is something I can't let happen, at least not until I get you back to your parents. Then they can figure out what to do with you." Rafe ran a hand through his blond hair.

As she stood there, KJ really looked at her oldest brother for the first time, and she could see the concern in his blue eyes, and the tension lining his angular face. His broad shoulders were set with irritation, and his muscles were tight as if he anticipated a fight from her. There was honesty in every line of his body, and her wolf wouldn't allow her to continue arguing. He was giving her more time to figure things out, so she would take it and appreciate it.

"Thank you. I just…I just can't deal with it right now. I need to get back to Mom and Dad and the rest of my family. I need to know she's okay."

He nodded and sighed as some of the stress in his stance eased. "I know. Get in the van. Ryley is headed this way and I'm sending your van on ahead. I want to run for a couple minutes before we load up in our van, but we'll follow shortly."

With that, he turned and headed down the same footpath that she had just walked, and disappeared into the trees. Cash and Noah appeared a moment later, and she heard Ryley opening the driver's side door on the other side of the van. Sighing with a combination of relief and disappointment when Thomas didn't reappear as well, she climbed into the van, and settled into her seat. Closing her eyes, she willed herself to sleep as the other three settled in and they hit the highway again in silence.

CHAPTER FOUR

The only sound was the vibration of the van, as Thomas, Owen, Rafe, and Luke resumed their drive. They were just a few minutes behind the first van, but it was driving Thomas crazy that he hadn't gone after KJ so he could spend more time with her. Thomas hadn't spoken to Noah and Luke after KJ walked away from them, choosing to walk the other direction, separating himself from everyone for a few minutes in order to calm his raging hard-on. His brain felt like mush, and his body was on fire. It was freaky how just a quick make out session with that woman had him ready to pin her to the nearest tree and fuck her silly.

He wanted to kick his own ass for molesting her so quickly. She was way too young for him, and now was not the time to be starting a wild affair, especially, when her brothers were big-ass werewolves who would rip him to pieces if he upset her. He needed to apologize to her and explain that they couldn't continue this crazy…well…whatever it was. They just couldn't continue.

Once he felt like he had his emotions under control, he had started back toward the van with the intention of finding KJ, only to find her and the other van gone. Luke and Owen had been waiting by the van, but Rafe was nowhere in sight.

When Thomas asked about the other group, Owen had explained that Rafe told them to go ahead while he ran for a minute in the woods before they headed back out. Although Thomas hated standing around waiting to get back to it, it had turned out to be worth it when Rafe came out of the woods in his wolf form, and Thomas got to see him shift.

These wolves were built magnificently, in either form. Seeing their bodies contort from one shape to another was like watching a sci-fi movie. The scientific doctor in him wanted to ask a million questions about how it worked and how it felt, but he sensed a change in the atmosphere between he and Rafe, so he kept his mouth shut.

Now they were back on the road, and all he had for company were his thoughts as the other three men were oddly silent ever since they loaded back up.

"So, what was that between you and KJ?" Luke asked, startling Thomas away from his musings. Thomas held the younger man's intense gaze for a few moments before shrugging his shoulders.

"I'm not sure, why?" he asked.

"She's a great girl, and I don't want to see you hurt her," Luke said sharply.

Thomas frowned. "Hurting her is the last thing I want to do."

"She's dealing with a lot of shit right now, so she doesn't need you hitting on her, too," Luke grumbled.

"Let's get one thing straight, Luke. You don't tell me who I can and can't hit on. I like KJ, and I have no bad intentions where she is concerned. I'm attracted to her, she's attracted to me, that's it. End of story. It doesn't mean that anything will come of it. Not that it's any of your business," Thomas said coldly.

Luke was starting to get on his nerves. The kid was wound tighter than a pocket watch and acted like he was some sort of guard dog for KJ. It wasn't like Thomas had done anything wrong, and KJ clearly wanted that kiss as much as he had.

"Everything about the pack is my business, human. You're the one who doesn't have any rights here." Luke's voice had changed with his anger, and it came out as a combination growl and snarl.

"Shut up, Luke. You're not KJ's babysitter. We have at least eight more hours in this car together, so cut the He-man act, would you?" Rafe said from the driver's seat.

After another hard look at Thomas over his shoulder, Luke huffed and then turned back around to glare out the front window. Thomas sighed with a combination of relief and irritation. He wished he could go back in time a half hour and change how that whole incident went down. Not that he would change kissing KJ, but he hated that the moment had been spoiled by such a harsh interruption. His balls still ached for release, and when he let himself remember the taste of her on his tongue and the feel of her in his arms his cock thickened in his jeans.

Inwardly cursing his body's reaction, he had to bite the inside of his cheek to keep from groaning out loud. No matter how many reasons he had to avoid her, there wasn't a chance in hell that he would be able to keep his distance from her now.

"Where did you go to school, Doc?" Owen asked, turning to face him.

"MU, where did you study law?"

"Kansas, on scholarship. Otherwise I probably wouldn't have gone at all."

Thomas grinned at him. "I know that feeling. I had a scholarship too, but I'm still paying out the ass on school loans."

"Everyone thinks doctors and lawyers have it made once they grad-uate, but it sure didn't work that way for me." Owen chuckled and shrugged.

"Why law school?"

"Lots of reasons, but I didn't want to be a full-time firefighter. I tried it for a year, and it was nice having all the female attention—women sure do like firemen—but it wasn't for me. I lost a friend in a fire my rookie year, and it messed me up. I knew I had to pick a different direction. I still volunteer, but I mainly just do the demonstration part now. No fighting fires for me."

"Shit, I'm sorry, man. I didn't mean to bring up bad memories."

"No, I'm past it for the most part, but I couldn't run into burning buildings after that."

"So are you the only one who isn't a career fireman?"

Rafe snorted from the front seat. "Not quite!"

Luke didn't even turn around to look at him when he spoke. "No, not all of us need to be heroes."

Thomas and Owen exchanged looks before Owen shook his head and shrugged. "Devin and Damon got on at the fire department first, and everyone else sort of just followed them. We've always been a tight-knit group, since we were all around the same age. We grew up together. Except for the couple years I remember the twins going to Memphis for school, we've been together. Even in the Marines we were in the same unit."

"Devin and Damon went to Memphis for school?"

"Yeah, there is a school there for werewolves specifically. The Eastern Pack School."

Thomas stared at Owen in disbelief. "Are you shitting me? A werewolf school?"

Luke growled from the front seat. "What, werewolves can't be educated now?"

"No. I was just a little surprised. You have to admit you're a secretive group, so to hear there was a school…Well, I'm just trying to figure out what the difference is between it and a regular school." Thomas was trying hard to rein in his automatic reaction to punch Luke in the face. What the hell was this guy's problem? He acted like Thomas was beneath him, and the way he had acted about KJ was ridiculous.

"Pack school is for Alpha heirs only. They go to basically get educated on the general werewolf society, and etiquette. If you ask Dev, it was one of the worst times in his life. He hated it," Rafe answered before Thomas or Luke could.

"I have so much to learn about you guys," Thomas said, dropping his head back onto the headrest of the seat.

"It'll come with time, Doc. Don't try to learn it all at once. You're moving in with us, so you'll be an expert in no time." Owen adjusted his own seat, and closed his eyes signaling the end of the conversation as the other two wolves didn't seem to want to chitchat either.

Forcing himself to close his own eyes, Thomas focused on blanking out his mind so he could get some rest. With hours left on their drive time, and a van mostly full of bitchy wolves, he couldn't think of a better option than to sleep through the trip.

Several hours later, Thomas woke to the sound of the van door shutting and realized that they had stopped. Glancing out the window he could see that they weren't at a rest stop but instead they were on a gravel road surrounded by trees. All three of the van's other occupants had gotten out, and as he climbed out too, he saw the other van parked a little way away.

Everyone was milling about chattering, except for KJ, who was perched on the back bumper of the first van, worrying her bottom lip with her teeth. Her beautiful hair was swept over one shoulder and hung in a waterfall over the ground as she rested her elbows on her knees. In that position she looked hardened and vulnerable all at once. He had an incessant urge to wrap her in his arms and promise to protect her forever. The moment he exited the vehicle, she jerked her head up and her gorgeous blue eyes met his. Even from twenty feet away he could see the need burning in them, and he started to move in her direction.

Before he could reach her, she jumped to her feet, and began walking into the woods, calling out, "I'm taking a run."

Irritation and pride kept Thomas from going after her. She was avoiding him. He hadn't done anything wrong, so why the hell would she avoid him?

"Doc?" He turned to look at Cash who was watching him with a cocked eyebrow. "We are going to take a run to burn off some energy before we go again. Do you mind waiting with the vans for a few minutes?"

Thomas nodded his agreement and watched as all the men began stripping their clothes off. A quick glance around him assured Thomas that the road they were on was deserted and looked rarely used. Hopefully rarely enough that no one would happen upon them and ask questions about why he had six piles of clothing and two vans and yet appeared to be alone.

The men shifted, and in a breath, they were all gone from view, leaving Thomas alone with his thoughts.

He kicked the tire of the van KJ had been riding in out of pure frustration. It was going to be impossible to figure out why there was such chemistry between the two of them, if he couldn't get her alone to talk. Of course, the moment he imagined having her alone, his cock hardened in his jeans, and his brain stopped functioning properly. He wanted her alone all right, but not to just talk. He wanted to get his hands and his mouth back on that soft little body.

A scraping noise behind him was his only warning, before a blinding flash of pain shot through his temple, and the world went black.

KJ had barely taken a step after her shift, before the wolf landed on her back. The air slammed out of her lungs, so she couldn't even yelp to warn the other wolves, and she was quickly muzzled and tied by human hands.

"There you are, my pretty. We've been chasing after you for weeks. Nico is going to be so pleased when we show up with you in hand." The man talking to her was a werewolf, she could smell it on him. She knew the Kaplan stench from any other scent, and she whined in her throat. "Yeah, you should probably be scared. I've heard that Nico's been wanting you for a long time, and he ain't very nice to his women. You're probably in for it with that wolf, he's a mean son of a bitch."

She was hoisted up onto the man's shoulder still in wolf form and carried through the woods to a waiting pickup truck. Two other men were waiting for them and they both grinned when he dumped her on the ground next to them. The taller of the two was leaning nonchalantly against the driver's side door frame. His eyes lit over her wolf, sparking with interest, and she growled a warning low in her throat.

"Good job, Jeff. Where's Ash?" The shorter man was ugly as sin, and KJ wished she could tell him so. These were the Kaplan Omegas that had been tailing her all the way to Kansas City. Her stomach turned as the scent of unwashed bodies overwhelmed her.

"He was supposed to be grabbing the human. Let's get her in the truck, that way when Ash gets here, we can move. Once those Grays catch our scent, they will be tracking us hard and fast. We have to get her back to Nico as soon as possible so he can mate her." The one named Jeff kept talking as he scooped her up again and dropped her in the back of the pickup truck.

Her heart was racing in her chest, as she processed what they were saying. Nicolas Kaplan was looking for her. Her? Not her mother? It didn't make any sense. And why would they want Thomas? Mate her? Nico wanted to mate her, holy shit! Before she could think any further on it, the sharp prick of a needle in her hip brought a whine to her throat as the warmth of some sort of drug slid through her blood.

"Nighty night, beautiful. When you wake up it will be in Nico's bed, so get some rest!"

The last thing she heard as she drifted into unconsciousness was the laughter of several men.

KJ came back to consciousness with the scent of her mate in her nose. Cracking her eyes open to look for Thomas, she was surprised to find herself alone in a large empty room. It was probably a living room, based on the door and window placement, but she really wasn't sure. She was in a metal cage, but she had shifted into human form at some point, and someone had left a pair of sweatpants and a T-shirt in the cage with her. Confusion blurred her brain as she dressed. She could smell her mate, but it was different than Thomas's earlier scent. Maybe it was the same drugs they had given her, sometimes medication changed a wolf's scent, so it was possible it did the same to humans.

She waited alone in the cage for what seemed like hours but was probably only minutes. She could hear the rumble of two voices sitting outside the front door, and she finally determined that it was Kaplan wolves guarding her. Thomas had to be nearby, but she didn't get a sense of him. The scent was coming from outside of the cabin, and she was beginning to fear that he was already dead.

Suddenly the door flung open, and a large man with long, white-blond hair, and a full mountain man beard and mustache, stood in front of her. His nearly black eyes were unsettling to say the least, and his scent made her blood freeze. This was Nicolas Kaplan. There was no doubt in her mind. His face might have been attractive if it weren't for the sneer marring it right now. He had a wide jaw, and a wide flat nose above full lips. The large scar just above his right eyebrow made him seem even more dangerous and a tremor of genuine fear rattled her spine.

"Well, well, well, we finally meet. Katie Jo, allow me to introduce myself, I'm Nicolas Kaplan, your future mate," he said with a leer and a chuckle.

"Fuck you," she snapped, "you are *not* my mate."

He laughed harder at her denial and then crouched down in front of the cage. "Not your bond mate maybe, but you *will* be my mate. I haven't come this far to walk away with nothing. I suppose you do have the option of being my slave. I'll leave the choice up to you."

He stood again and fished a key from the pocket of his black jeans. She took a second to size him up and felt nauseous again. Nicolas was at least six-foot-tall and outweighed her by a good hundred pounds. He was built like a house, wide all the way down and packed with muscle. It would be suicide to fight him, but there was no way in hell she would willingly give herself up to him either.

"I'll let you out of the cage if you promise to be a good girl. You don't want to know what happens if you're not. Can you manage?" Nicolas said, eyeing her speculatively.

"I wouldn't open the cage if I were you." She snarled, "The moment I have a chance I'm going to rip your fucking throat out."

Anger flared in his eyes, but his lips quirked up in a grin. "Oh, I do love a woman with spirit. I can't wait to put you on your back and... teach you a lesson, my venomous little bitch."

She growled at him which only seemed to encourage his evil pleasure. This was craziness. Since when did Nicolas Kaplan want her and not her mother?

"What do you want with me? I thought you wanted my mom?" she asked, hoping the question would delay him from his goal.

"Tasha? Oh I never wanted *her*, I just wanted the gold claim her daddy was planning on leaving to her. She's worth a fortune, well, she was worth a fortune. I've also found that my stamina requires younger blood. Tasha couldn't keep up with me now, and at this point she's used goods after three kids. But she took the choice out of my hands by running away from me, so I'm paying her back by taking the choice out of yours. Won't it just please Mommy and Daddy to welcome their new son-in-law into the pack?" He chuckled again and crouched back down by the cage door. Reaching a hand in, he smiled wider when she slapped his hand away from her.

"It won't happen, Kaplan. You'll have to kill me, because I won't mate with you," she said, and he cocked his head.

"Why not? I'm the Beta to one of the strongest packs in the country. You can't do better than me." He didn't seem angry so much as intrigued.

"I'm already mated."

"No, you're not. I checked for a mark when my men turned you over to me. You're unclaimed."

"He hasn't claimed me yet, but he will. You don't want to be standing in his way when he finds me," she said, tilting her chin defiantly.

"I hope he comes looking. I'm itching for a good fight. In fact, I'm hoping those Gray Pack wolves decide to play hero and come looking for you, but for the moment I'll settle for a good hard fuck to ease my stress." His hand snaked inside the cage, and gripped her by the hair, jerking her forward so her cheek slammed into the bars. "I'm going to open the cage, and you're going to play nice, or I will leave you in so much pain you won't remember your own name, got it?"

She blinked back tears from the burning pain in her scalp. There was no way she would be able to fight him off. He was going to rape her, and there wasn't shit she could do. Where the fuck was Thomas, and where were the other Gray wolves?

The key clicked in the lock, and the metal cage door popped open. Nicolas released her hair long enough to reach in with the other arm, and grip her wrist, yanking her forward and out of the cage. She slid, trying to get to her feet and landed on her knees with a gasp of pain.

Nicolas gave her a lewd grin, and then released his hold on her to reach for his zipper. "Well, since you're down there, I suppose we'll just take advantage—"

A sharp knock on the door cut his words off and had KJ breathing a sigh of relief. There was no way she could suck his dick without biting the fucker. Whomever the intruder was had likely saved her life, because Nicolas would kill her the moment, she sunk her teeth into his flesh.

"What the fuck is it?" Nicolas snarled, turning toward the door.

"The human is awake, and he says he's a doctor."

The voice behind the closed door washed over KJ with surprising heat. It was low and had a delicious rasp to it, and it belonged to a stranger. What the hell was wrong with her? She was lusting after a stranger's voice now! Her life was totally freaking screwed up.

"I'll deal with him in a minute," Nicolas yelled.

"But, Nico, Allen needs that buckshot out of his hide so he can shift." Nicolas was silent for a moment, but KJ could see his brain thinking through the risk of leaving his pack mate injured.

"Fuck. Fine, I'm coming." Nicolas grabbed her by the shoulders and pulled her to her feet. Compared to his large frame she was very petite. Thomas made her feel protected in the shadow of his muscular body, but Nicolas made her feel vulnerable. A tremor of true fear hit her. This was a man that was evil all the way to the core. If he wanted to, he could break her in half. "I'll deal with you in a little while. Don't worry, my pretty pet, we'll resume right where we left off."

KJ yelped as he dropped her to the floor without warning. Her legs buckled underneath her, and she went down hard. Disoriented, she wasn't able to get a glimpse of the man outside the cabin door before Nicolas slammed it shut behind him.

She could hear him speaking to whoever was outside about taking her to another cabin, but then their voices were muffled, and she growled with frustration. Fuck a duck this whole thing was going to get worse. Whoever stood outside that door with Nicolas was making her wolf howl just by being close.

Two sets of footsteps moved away, and the scent dissipated. The stranger had made it sound like Thomas was a way away from her, so why was she scenting the mating lust? Was it possible that she had two mates? What if the stranger was also her mate? A nervous growl rumbled from her wolf, and she nearly vomited. Two mates were three times worse in this case, and she needed to get the hell out of here before Nicolas came back.

CHAPTER FIVE

$\mathcal{T}$he cabin she was in was empty, and completely secure as far as she could tell. The windows were boarded up from the outside, and the doors were securely locked. No matter how much she searched for a weakness in the wooden walls, she was locked in an unbreakable cage. The awkward fit of the men's T-shirt and sweat-pants was driving her mad as she continuously had to pull them up from her knees, and her anxiety and frustration made her pace the perimeter of the front room. Every now and then she would get a whiff of the other male that her wolf desperately wanted her to go to, but she couldn't pick up on Thomas's scent at all. It was very confus-ing. Ultimately, she settled on the floor with her back to the metal bars of the open cage, facing the front door, and praying that her brothers wouldn't leave her in Kaplan hands for very long.

What seemed like hours later, she was startled from a restless doze, when the door finally flung open, and a large male wolf came in with Thomas thrown over his shoulder. KJ bit her tongue to keep from whimpering when he dropped Thomas to the ground without concern for his person. That landing was going to bruise tomorrow.

With her eyes on Thomas's unconscious form, she missed seeing the male wolf move in her direction until his hand wrapped around the back of her neck. He lifted her to her feet, gripping her so hard that she figured she would have her own set of bruises to match the ones on Thomas. His breath was wretched, and it turned her stomach when his cold, yellow eyes skimmed over her.

"You sure are a pretty bitch. You know, if Nico wasn't so bent on having you for his own, I would fuck you until I broke you," he said with a low snarl in his throat.

Trying not to let her fear show, she growled back. "It's more likely that I would break you before your pecker got hard you nasty dog."

Her words hit their mark because he reacted instantly, throwing her to the floor and kicking her in the ribs. "I hope Nico kills you when he breeds you."

With that he stormed out the door, leaving her coughing as she gasped to refill her lungs with oxygen. She scooted over to where Thomas was. His face was pale, and he had a huge black and blue bruise on his cheek as well as one swollen eye. By the look of his clothing, he had put up one hell of a fight at some point, and a wave of pride washed over her, that this strong man was her mate.

Immediately her stomach flip-flopped. What was she saying? Was she already accepting the mating? Looking back at the beaten man stretched out limply on the floor, she sighed heavily. How could she not accept the mating? The only reason that Thomas was even here in… well, wherever they ended up, was because of her. For the first time she truly looked at him from top to bottom. His dark brown hair was nearly black in color, but streaks of amber highlighted it here and there. It had a wavy curl to it that made it look messy all the time. High cheekbones and a square jaw gave his profile an angular, masculine look. His shoulders were broad and his chest wide, but she had picked up on that when he held her against him. Where his T-shirt pulled up out of his jeans, she could see the light dusting of dark black hairs on his muscular abs, and she wondered if that line went all the way up, and then if it went all the way down.

Her wolf howled in her head and her mouth watered at the

thought. His lean hips had etched muscles carved into them that matched that line of hair perfectly, so in essence there was an arrow pointing straight to the large bulge under his zipper. Taunting her. Giving a huff of frustration when she caught the scent of her own desire, she closed her eyes against the delectable view, and focused on regaining her control.

Once she felt like she had herself in check, she reopened her eyes and pressed her hand to his wrist to check his pulse. It was still strong and steady, but her wolf wouldn't let her leave his side at this point, so she curled up against him. His scent filled her nose and warmed her from the inside out. Anxiety rolled in her belly over what would happen to the two of them but having Thomas with her gave her a tiny grain of hope that they might get out of there alive.

"KJ?" Thomas stared down at the woman who rested on his chest. He could feel his whole body responding to holding her close. "KJ, what's going on? Where are we? And what are you wearing?"

He watched with a frown as she came awake slowly, and then sat up with a start. She glanced down at the oversized T-shirt that had pulled down over her shoulder while she slept. It bared most of her cleavage and throat to his view, and a pink blush crept over her cheeks before she lifted her eyes back to his. "The Kaplan wolves got me while I was in wolf form. My clothes were back at the van and based on the uses that Nicolas Kaplan has already outlined for me, I don't suspect I will be getting a new wardrobe any time soon. I'm lucky to have this."

"Shit. I remember. They took me, and they beat the shit out of me before they realized they had a use for me. They made me take the buckshot out of some guy's ass so he could shift into his wolf form to heal. That's a hard task to do with one eye swollen almost shut."

Jealousy was burning in his gut. She was wearing some schmuck's shirt, and by the look of the bruise on her throat whoever it was had hurt her. He sat up with a groan and pulled his shirt off. The light of desire glowed from her pretty blue eyes as they skimmed over his chest and zeroed in on his zipper, and he nearly threw the shirt to the side to pull her back against him. Instead he forced himself to hand it to her.

She frowned in confusion. "What are you doing?"

"Please? Just wear mine instead. I can't stand to think that you're wearing the clothes of someone who hurt you."

"It's no big deal—" She started to protest.

"Please, just this once don't argue."

He ground his teeth together while he waited for her to decide, and then when she finally did he had to bite his tongue to keep from groaning. She whipped the huge stranger's shirt and sweats off and threw the clothing across the room. He took in her gorgeous curves just before the T-shirt settled over them, and instantly his cock was as hard as concrete.

"Did they get anyone else?" Her face was drawn and pinched with worry, and he pulled her into his lap, sighing with pleasure as she buried her face in his neck, and locked her arms around his waist.

"I didn't see anyone else. Cash and the others went into the woods on the opposite side of the road after you took off. They were trying to give you some space," he answered, pressing a kiss to the crown of her head. Her blonde hair was silky, and he stroked his fingers through it, petting her gently.

"This is all my fault! If I had just talked to you, and not acted like a child—" Her voice caught on a sob, and his heart broke.

"Shh…little one, they were waiting for us. If it hadn't been now, they would have gotten us later. It's not your fault at all."

"We have to figure out a way out of this." Her breath was warm over his collarbone, and his balls ached. He knew that she could feel his hard cock under her ass, but she was ignoring it.

"KJ, Nico—I mean Nicolas Kaplan—said that he is going to keep me for the moment because I'm useful, but those wolves are blood-thirsty. I'm not sure how long he will hold them off killing me just for the fun of it. I'm guessing they took you to use against your mom and dad."

"No, Kaplan was in here earlier. He said that he plans to keep me as his mate, and he said something about a gold claim that my grandfather had."

"Gold?" he asked doubtfully.

"Yeah, it was the strangest thing because I've never heard my parents even mention anything about gold or my grandfather being wealthy. He said that he wanted my mom initially to get his hands on the gold, but now she's too old for him. Apparently, he has decided that I will do in her place." Her eyes lifted to meet his, and her face was a scary white color. Fear was etched in every line of her frown, and Thomas wanted to kill the wolf that scared her so much.

KJ's eyes suddenly widened, and she held her finger up to signal him to be quiet, as she moved out of his lap. The sound of footsteps outside the front door snagged his attention, and he froze, holding his breath. The person hesitated, and then the sound of a key in the lock sent goose bumps prickling over Thomas's skin. This was it. The Kaplan wolves were coming for them. Jumping to his feet, he braced himself behind the door, prepared to attack the intruder before they could get fully into the room.

When the door opened, Thomas launched himself at the male body, and had him in a choke hold before he could move much. The blond man's hands went up instinctively to grab ahold of Thomas's arm, and the next thing he knew, he was slamming into the floor on his back.

Fuck, these wolves were strong, was all he could think as he struggled to drag oxygen back into his lungs. His body vibrated with the intense impact of the floor, and stars winked in his vision.

"Shit. Damn it, man. Do you have to go trying to be a hero? I could have killed you. Stupid human. Get up, quick. We have to move fast if we're going to get out of here before Nico finds out we're gone."

To Thomas's utter amazement, the blond man with bright green eyes moved across the room with a set of keys in his hand and reached his hand out to help KJ to her feet. She jerked away, and the man sighed with frustration.

"Do you want out of here or not, mate?" he growled at her.

"Mate?" Thomas gaped at their rescuer, and a blushing KJ.

"I know you smell it. Let me get you out of here safely, and then we can talk. We have to hurry." The man didn't even acknowledge Thomas as he helped KJ stand, but he frowned when she immediately moved to Thomas's side, and helped him rise to his feet as well. Thomas could see the confusion in her blue eyes, as she swept her gaze over him and the new man. She seemed to be so surprised she was speechless, and for once Thomas was, too.

Jealousy rumbled in his chest at the idea of this new man calling her his mate. KJ was his. He'd be damned if this blond asshole was going to come in and sweep her away with some sort of werewolf endearment. The man was right about one thing, they had to get out of here while they had the chance.

Thomas wrapped his arm around KJ's shoulders and used his fingertip to lift her chin so she could look at him. "Are you okay with this, little one?"

She nodded, still looking puzzled, and slightly frazzled. "Yes, he's right, we have to trust him. It's the only chance we've got." She glanced back at their rescuer, who gave her a nod that grated Thomas's nerves.

Much to his dismay, she whipped his T-shirt off right there in front of them both and shifted into her wolf form. Thomas took a chance and glanced at his rival while she was naked. The look of pure lust in his green eyes nearly got the man killed, but somehow Thomas managed to rein his jealousy in as he tugged his shirt back on. Her smell filled his nose, and he could still feel the warmth of her body in the fabric. Soothed, he was able to face the two of them, and give a begrudging nod.

With KJ in wolf form, and he and the stranger on foot, they all made their way down the hallway of the house they were being held in. The house was smaller than Thomas originally thought, and before he knew it they stood at a back door. The man stopped before he inserted the key into the lock.

"We are going to have to make a run for it. Can you keep up, human?" Thomas glared back at the man, and then gave a sharp nod just before the man jerked the door open. "Good, I'm not waiting for you. She's my sole priority right now."

With those parting words the man pulled his clothes off, looping them around his neck, and then he shifted into an enormous white wolf, and used his nose to nudge KJ out the now-open door. The two wolves took off at a run across the small yard toward the woods, and all Thomas could do was follow them. His heart was pounding in his chest as he ran into the dim tree line. Expecting to hear a call of alarm or the snarling and snapping of deadly wolves, Thomas ran his heart out. He pushed himself to run faster and harder than he ever had in his life.

He managed to keep up for the most part with the two wolves, but he knew that was only because the two of them weren't running at full speed. KJ kept turning her golden head to check that he was still with them, and the strange wolf kept circling back behind them as though assuring himself that they weren't being followed. They ran for several minutes, and if Thomas had to guess, at least a couple miles, before his body began to slow. Adrenaline drained from him, and he came to a stop, bending over with his hands on his knees gasping for air.

The two wolves noticed quickly and turned back to come to his side. The white wolf sat on his haunches panting while the vivid green of his eyes scanned the trees behind them. KJ shifted as soon as she was close to Thomas, and she reached out for him.

"Are you okay, Thomas?" she said as she worked to catch her own breath.

"Fine," he snapped, jerking his shirt back off and throwing it at her. "Would you please put something on?"

She let out a sharp laugh that rang of nerves and began to dress. Thomas noticed that the white wolf kept his gaze locked on her nudity the whole time it was in view, and he waited until she was covered to shift back into his human form.

"Who are you?" KJ asked, staring at the naked stranger, who did nothing in the way of redressing.

"Bryson Samuels. Until a few moments ago, I was an Omega with the Kaplan Pack. I don't think they would like it if I called myself that now, after betraying my pack Alpha to get you two out of there." Bryson gave them both a crooked grin, and KJ frowned.

"Why did you do it?" she looked like she already knew the answer, and Thomas dreaded Bryson's response.

"You're my mate. I knew it the moment I caught your scent. I had to." Bryson shrugged, and returned her frown with a steady gaze.

Thomas nearly laughed out loud, as he realized he was chatting with the mate of the woman he wanted to seduce, while the man was completely naked. He couldn't resist taking a quick peek at Bryson's assets, and though the man wasn't lacking in the physical department, Thomas wasn't at a complete disadvantage there either.

"I don't know what you're talking about." KJ whispered the words, but it was clear by the uncomfortable tension between them, that she knew exactly what he was talking about.

"So, you're saying that KJ is your mate, and because you smelled her and realized it, you risked your life to rescue us," Thomas said, trying to make sure he had all the facts straight.

"Way to go, wizzo. You catch on quick, but I wasn't rescuing you, I was rescuing her, and you just happened to luck out by being kept in the same room with her," Bryson said with a shrug. That shrug of his was really getting on Thomas's nerves, and he ground his teeth to keep from punching the cocky bastard.

"No. She's mine." The words were out of Thomas's mouth before he could stop them. KJ groaned, and Bryson growled. Thomas fully expected her to deny his claim considering they had only kissed once, and he really had no right to be so possessive of her, but she surprised him by putting her head in her hands and talking to herself.

"Why me? Really? It's not enough that I've spent my whole life on the run, hiding from some psychotic bastard that wants to fuck my mom, but now fate has to throw me a fucking curveball like this. This is just not my fucking day."

"Watch your mouth," Thomas snapped, and her blue eyes lifted to meet his. The anger in her gaze was expected, but what surprised him was the fear that lit their depths. "Now what the hell are you talking about?"

"Oh, so you can curse, but I can't? Well isn't that just like a man," she said snottily, and Thomas was even more surprised to hear Bryson growl.

"Watch it, ice. The human is right, you shouldn't speak like that, it doesn't sound good coming from a woman." Bryson's words seemed to trigger something in KJ, and she let out a small shriek of irritation.

"You two are both dumbasses, and to think I'm stuck with the two of you. I had to have done something really bad in a previous life." She spun on her heel and stalked away from them.

"Stop," Thomas snapped. When she stopped with her back still facing them, he glanced at Bryson who looked just as confounded as he was. "What do you mean you're stuck with the *two* of us?"

He watched her shoulders rise and fall with a sigh, and she tipped her head back, so she was looking up into the trees. "You're both my mates."

"What the hell?"

"Fuck." Thomas's brain was spinning, and he stared at the back of her blonde head. "When did you know?"

She remained quiet, but Bryson didn't. "What the fuck do you mean, we're *both* your mates? How can we both be your mate?"

"It seems to be happening frequently in the Gray Pack," Thomas said softly, as he met Bryson's shocked green eyes. "The Alpha and his twin brother are mated to the same woman, and there is at least one other trio that is mated. I take it that it's not a normal werewolf relationship?"

Bryson shook his head and lowered himself to the ground to sit. Thomas was relieved because for a minute it looked like the man might pass out. At least this way he wouldn't fall very far.

Stepping over to KJ, he turned her around, and tipped her head back so she was looking up into his eyes. She looked resigned and terrified all at once, and Thomas had the urge to clutch her against his chest and soothe her. He wanted nothing more than to ease her anxiety, but right now his own emotions were running on edge.

"Katie Jo, when did you know I was your mate?" he asked again, more softly this time.

She was quiet for another second before she blew out a deep breath, and muttered, "The moment we met."

Thomas's hiss of breath and the pain on his face shot through KJ's core. She felt terrible for hurting him, but he had to know the truth. Even now she could feel the mating lust surging through her body being this close to the two of them, and it was making her head hurt. She had never imagined that she might end up with two mates, but her wolf was prancing inside of her, desperate to touch them both.

"So, what now? I'm just supposed to agree to share my mate with a fucking human?" Bryson growled from his place on the forest floor. His body was tense with anger, and his face was pale from shock.

She studied the blond man seriously for the first time, and her heart beat faster. He was a couple inches shorter than Thomas, but a little bit bulkier. His chest and broad shoulders were ripped with muscles and her wolf wanted to lick every one of them. There was a jagged scar down his right side over his ribs, and her fingers itched to explore the puckered skin. His green eyes, unlike any she had ever seen, were a brilliant peridot color. The white wolf form wasn't much of a surprise considering his blond hair was so light in color it was nearly white. He had thick blond eyebrows, and a narrow Roman nose above full lips and a sharp jaw. The deep dimple in his chin gave him a cocky appearance as he sat there returning her perusal.

"Do you think I have a choice?" she snapped. "I don't even want one mate, much less two of them. I have plans for my life, and they do not involve being strapped to two chauvinistic, arrogant assholes."

She shoved at Thomas's chest, pushing him away from her, and turned her back on the two of them, so they wouldn't see the tears that spilled from her eyes. She began walking again, refusing to just sit and wait for the Kaplan wolves to find them and haul her back to be Nicolas's chew toy. It wasn't even a full minute before a hand on her arm stopped her. Without looking up, she froze, and waited. The hand slid up to her shoulders, and Bryson's broad body stepped into her view. Since both of his hands were in view, that meant that the hands on her shoulders were...

She jumped when Thomas pressed against her back, and lightly brushed the top of her head with a kiss. Did he know how much she liked that? Meanwhile Bryson took her face in his hands and held her still. He stared down into her teary eyes, looking confused and anxious.

"Wait a second, peaches. I don't know why fate deemed to put two of us with you, but I do know that my wolf isn't going to let me give you up. Terminator here may not have a wolf inside of him, but he doesn't look like he's stepping down either, so we'll make this work, somehow." His green eyes flicked up to look at Thomas behind her, and she felt his body relax slightly at whatever he saw. "We all need a little time to adjust to this, but first things first, we need to get out of here, and find someplace safe."

"We have to get to Quiver Creek. That's where we were going," KJ said, letting her eyes drift closed as her body responded to being between the two men. Her heart was racing, and her stomach was dancing with butterflies. She knew that the smell of her own arousal would trigger Bryson's wolf to react, but she had no idea if Thomas would be aware of her desire.

"Ice, you're going to have to stop thinking with your hormones, or I'm going to end up mating you in the dirt like an animal," Bryson ground out, and her eyes flew up to his face. His jaw was set, and a muscle ticked in it. Pressed against her belly was the evidence of his words, and her thighs were suddenly damp with need. She shoved at his chest, which only succeeded in pushing her ass back against Thomas's matching erection.

Oh my god, I'd give anything to have him do just that to me, she thought, and heard herself growl in frustration. She was torn between begging them both to mate her and running away from them both until her legs gave out. Settling for option C, she stepped from between them, and rubbed at her sweaty palms. "I'm sorry, it's biological, not a conscious choice."

Bryson grabbed her hand and pressed his lips to her still damp palm. "No worries, peaches, once you get to know me, it will always be a conscious choice." His flirty smile had her smiling back, and she shook her head as Thomas snorted.

"Good grief. You're standing here flirting while a pack of angry wolves is on our tail. Any chance we could find somewhere to hole up for the night? It's going to get dark, and we need to figure out how to connect with the rest of the Gray wolves that were with us when we got captured. Bryson, do you know if any others were taken?" Thomas asked, running his hand through his messy brown hair. KJ thought that the little gesture was ridiculously adorable and had to turn away from him. Staring into the woods in the direction they had just come from, she took a deep breath hoping to catch the scent of any other wolves in the area.

"No, it was just the two of you, her because we were ordered to get her, and you because you were human and with a pack of wolves. Nico wanted to know what was so fascinating about you that they would keep you like a pet."

"I'm no fucking pet! I'm a doctor, in fact I'm the pack doctor, and since apparently I'm sharing your mate somehow, I'm about to be your family," Thomas snapped. KJ's stomach tightened even further, and she rolled her eyes when Bryson frowned back at him. "Do you know why Nico ordered KJ kidnapped?"

"Nope, but I was just muscle, so no one ever told me more than I needed to know."

"Why doesn't that surprise me?" Thomas said snarkily, and KJ huffed at him.

"Enough, you two! Bryson Samuels, meet Thomas Jameson. The only human to ever have complete access to the Gray Pack werewolves, and someone I trust implicitly. Get used to him being around, or feel free to head back the way we came. Thomas, Bryson is my mate too, I don't understand it, but I can't change it. And if I have to deal with it, then so do you, otherwise, you can get to stepping too." She stood between the two men again, but this time she felt like a barrier instead of a connector, and she crossed her arms around her breasts defiantly.

When both men nodded slowly, she sighed with relief, "Thank you. Now, Bryson, do you know where we are, and if there is somewhere we can stay for the night?"

"Yeah, we're in Sterling State Park, just outside Sterling, Colorado. The town is probably three miles west of us," Bryson said, giving her a look of apology.

"Then let's hike there and see about finding some shelter for the night, and maybe some food? I'm starving," KJ said, glancing over her shoulder. "Are you okay with that, Thomas?"

He nodded, taking a step closer, and placing one arm around her shoulders when he saw her shiver. He pressed a gentle kiss to her temple, and another piece of her armor melted. The sun was setting, and if they were going to make it to town before it got dark, they needed to get a move on. With a sigh, Bryson shifted back into his wolf, and then looked up at her expectantly.

"KJ, you need to shift, little one. You'll be warmer, and faster. If those Kaplan wolves catch up to us, you have to stay with Bryson and find the others. I can only go so fast on two feet, but if you guys get away, you can send help back for me," Thomas said, staring into her eyes. Her heart fluttered again. He was willing to sacrifice himself to help her escape and get back to her parents. It was unsettling and comforting all at once, and she offered him a smile.

"Okay, but hang on to this T-shirt, I'm starting to get attached to it." She tugged it off over her head, and grinned wider when his eyes slid down her naked frame, pausing at her breasts, and then again at the curls covering her pussy. "Hey! Doc! Eyes up top!"

He smirked at her and ran his tongue over his bottom lip as he met her gaze. "You can't blame me for getting a good look. You keep flashing it at me, and I won't be able to keep my hands off much longer."

She shivered, and shifted into her wolf form without responding, but she chuffed when he chuckled and she heard him whisper, "Chicken."

CHAPTER SIX

"Okay, I've managed to get us a room at the back. They didn't even ask to check ID, they took Bryson's credit card without even looking at it. I don't think anyone will believe I own two four-foot-tall dogs, so you guys are going to have to go in human form. KJ I can give you my shirt, so you're covered." Thomas frowned down at the large white wolf, who chuffed out a negative response and looked irritated. "You know, not everyone is comfortable wandering around completely naked, and I certainly don't want everyone checking her out as she walks through the parking lot."

He stripped off his shirt just as KJ shifted and handed it to her. His body instantly responded to her nudity, and he forced himself to look away. It hurt that she seemed to believe the only thing drawing him to her was biology. Just based on what little he knew of her at the moment, he still would have wanted her without the wolf lust thing. He only questioned whether or not she would have wanted him without her wolf telling her that they were mates?

"Okay, let's go, I want to call Devin as soon as possible. I don't know Ryley's cell number, but I remember Devin's." KJ didn't even meet his eyes, before she began walking across the parking lot. Thomas took off after her, leaving Bryson to shift and dress quickly to keep up.

The tired trio made their way across the parking lot to the back of the motel. The curtains were all drawn in the windows of the dozen or so rooms, and there were no vehicles in the lot. A vandalized dumpster was the only object of any bulk within view, but Thomas's nerves still jittered. He hadn't been prepared for the first attack, but they wouldn't take him by surprise again.

Once in the motel room, Bryson grabbed KJ's hand, and led her over to the phone, before taking a seat on one of the two double beds, while she began dialing.

"Hey, do you think we can get something delivered to eat when she's done? I'm starving," Bryson said, and Thomas felt like growling at him. He had to keep reminding himself that Bryson was a werewolf and could probably rip his throat out before he even managed to throw his arms up in defense. It was awfully hard to keep his temper in check when Bryson was holding KJ's hand like that. Any response he might have had was cut off, when KJ started talking.

"Devin? Hey it's KJ. Yeah, we're okay, they kicked the shit out of the doc…No, I think he's all right…He seems like he can take a licking and keep on ticking…. How did we get away? Well, that's kind of a funny story, and I really don't have time to tell it right now. We need the guys to come and get us. Yeah…and Devin…there are three of us…Well, see that's part of that long story…Okay, thanks. We'll check in with you once we're back with the rest of the pack. Bye."

KJ hung up the phone and visually deflated. Her body shrunk into itself as she pulled her hand away from Bryson and hugged her knees to her chest. Suddenly she looked very young, and very scared. Thomas's heart ached, and he moved to sit on the bed in front of her.

"It's going to be okay, little one, as soon as the rest of the crew can come and get us, we'll haul ass to get to Quiver Creek. The sooner we can get everyone loaded up and delivered safely to Kansas City the better." He ran his hand over her hair and tipped her chin. Her sky-blue eyes were filled with unshed tears, and her full lips were swollen from where her tiny white teeth kept chewing at them nervously. All he could think about was kissing away her fear and anguish, but the were-wolf next to her kept him from acting on it.

"I think it's time to clear the air a little bit, peaches. I know who you are by name, but since Fate seems to have thrown us all together, and I'm fighting my wolf to maintain control, we should probably talk about how this is going to work." For once Bryson was being reason-able instead of sarcastic, and Thomas nodded.

"Like she told you, I'm Thomas Jameson, the Gray Pack doctor. My younger sister, Tina, is a member of the pack." He held out his hand, which Bryson took in a firm grip.

"I would like to say it's nice to meet you, Tom, but I'm not sure that that's true just yet. What do you mean your sister is part of the pack? Is she human too?"

"She was, but when she met her mate, Liam, and mated with him she changed into a werewolf. From what I understand the biting during the mating starts a physiological shift in a human's DNA. It doesn't happen from just a regular werewolf bite, but the mating bond changes things," Thomas answered, but he kept his focus on KJ. She sat staring at the paisley bedspread next to her, without acknowledging the conversation the two men were having, and her continued silence was concerning. "Little one, are you okay? Did Nicolas hurt you?"

She shook her head. "No, I'm okay. I'm just overwhelmed."

The two men exchanged glances, and something clicked between them. They were both there for her, and whatever cultural and ideo-logical differences they had between them, they were going to work together to protect KJ, and make her happy.

"Are you hungry? Tom and I can order in some food if you want to take a shower while we wait for the rest of your pack." Bryson placed his hand on her knee, and she stared at it blankly. "Or, I can help you wash your back, while we wait for the food. Little scrap like you, washing your back wouldn't take too long, but I can't promise that it's the only part I'll put my hands on…"

His playful flirtation seemed to break through KJ's barrier, and she blushed pink. Rolling her eyes at him she snorted before replying, "Thanks, but no thanks. I'm not giving you an opportunity to lose control of your bodily urges. I'll be out in twenty minutes. By the way, I like meat on my pizza."

Her bare legs unfolded, and Thomas got a glorious glimpse of the blonde curls between her thighs before she stood and headed for the bathroom.

Bryson let out a loud belly laugh as she walked away. "There's the Ice Queen we know and love. You better be careful that your smart tongue doesn't overload your cute ass, ice."

"Thick crust, boys, with extra cheese!" The door clicked shut behind her, and Thomas heard the lock snick into place. Turning back to Bryson, they shared a grin between them.

"So, two mates, huh?"

Thomas nodded as his smile slipped from his face. "Yeah, so it seems. But—"

Bryson pulled the phone book out of the drawer of the nightstand and began flipping through it. "But what?"

"I'm human. Why would fate put her with me, when you can protect her better than I can?" Thomas asked. He could hear the frustration and doubt in his own voice, and he jumped up to pace the room. His agitated nerves wouldn't let him settle, and he prowled the room while Bryson ordered the pizza. The silence was deafening when Bryson hung up the phone and turned to watch Thomas's movements.

"From what I've already seen, our girl needs more than one mate to keep her safe. And if what you told me is right, you won't be human long. When you mate with KJ you will change, right?" Bryson asked.

Thomas froze in his tracks and stared at the bathroom door. Bryson was right. Being KJ's mate meant he would have to give up his human life and change into a werewolf. "Shit. How does the mating thing work?"

"Umm...didn't you say you were a doctor? What did they teach you in medical school?"

Thomas rolled his eyes, as he sat down at the small table. "I don't need you to teach me about sex, dumbass, how does the werewolf mating…er…*bond*…happen? What exactly is the mating lust?"

Bryson shifted so he was lying back on the bed propped up on his elbows and looked at Thomas skeptically. "Your sister is a werewolf, so she had to have bonded with her mate, and you're telling me you never thought to ask her how it worked?"

"It's my sister for God's sake! In my head she's still a six-year-old with pigtails and two missing front teeth. I don't even want to imagine her and Liam—" Thomas shuddered. "Just answer the question please?"

"Werewolf mating is done in three parts. The first is the mating lust. It's an unquenchable thirst for the other person. You crave touching them, tasting them, being close to them. I never believed the urge would be so strong, but nearly the instant KJ was brought in and I caught her scent I was rock hard and desperate to get to her. Like I told her, I'm battling my wolf right now to keep from rushing that bathroom door and fucking her against the wall. Damn, she's got a hot body, and those eyes…She's gorgeous!"

Thomas adjusted his own hard cock and glanced at the still closed door. "Yeah, I'm not sure she would appreciate the thought right now. She doesn't seem to be reacting to us the way we're reacting to her."

"Oh yeah she is. She's just fighting it. I saw her cheeks flush pink when we had her between us earlier, and the scent of her arousal is frying my brain. Trust me, she's feeling it, too. Anyway, the second part is the sex. It's supposed to be the most mind-blowing sex you can even imagine when it's between two true mates. It would probably be like a nuclear meltdown with three…" Bryson frowned again and sat up with his fists clenched. Even if they had come to some sort of peaceful agreement between the two of them, it still wasn't going to be easy to share a woman with a stranger. "The last piece of the puzzle is the bite. Werewolves mark each other with a bite—usually on the shoulder or neck. It's supposed to happen during sex, but I know of couples that marked each other without the sex."

"The biting is when the change is triggered in humans. That much

I do know. Why the neck or the shoulder? I've seen Tina's mark, and Caroline, the Gray Pack's Alpha Bitch, has two matching marks." Thomas couldn't imagine marring KJ's snow white skin with a scar from a sex bite. It seemed demeaning to her, and slightly disgusting to him.

"Werewolves maintain a traditional culture. We go by scent, and by ownership. I know it sounds bad, but mates own each other in our world. The bite mark is a claim of ownership on your mate, proof to everyone, especially other males, that she has been claimed. Once the mating is done, our scents change. It's obvious to me when I walk up to a woman that is mated because she smells like her mate. And vice versa, males take on some of their female's scent." Bryson stood and moved to the door. "Pizza's here."

"I don't hear anything?" Thomas questioned, but he accepted the cash Bryson handed him to pay for the food.

"That's because the car just turned into the parking lot. It will be at our door in about two minutes." Bryson shrugged when Thomas gave him a quizzical look. "Wolf hearing, man, another perk of the wolf."

The proof was in the pudding when a knock sounded a minute or so later and Thomas paid the delivery guy for the pizzas. Bryson went to the bathroom door and knocked lightly.

"Hey, Goldilocks, are you clean yet? Pizza is here."

KJ tugged the door open to face a grinning hunk of blond man, and she narrowed her eyes at him. "Goldilocks? I think you better get your fairy tales straight. Little Red Riding Hood had to deal with the wolf, not Goldilocks. She had bears—God help the girl." Tightening her grip on the tiny hotel bath towel that was wrapped around her body, she stepped out into the room.

Thomas was standing a few feet away with a pizza box in his hand and a lust-glazed look on his face. His jaw was slack, and his nostrils flared, making her pussy contract with need. Bryson stood inches away, so she could feel the heat rolling off him, and her wolf pranced inside of her, butting against her chest with a desperate need to reach out to her mates. Clenching her teeth, she closed her eyes and took a deep breath to clear her head. Immediately, she realized her mistake, as the scent of aroused male filled her nose, and a moan slipped from her throat.

"Are you okay, little one?" Thomas was instantly at her side, running his hands over her, checking for injuries. Her eyes popped open to meet his concerned gaze, and she choked on her own tongue. Too close. Too much. They were just too much to handle right now.

She took a step backward and stumbled, but both men caught her, holding her upright. Bryson with one arm wrapped around her waist, and Thomas with both hands in his large grip. Standing between their two muscular forms, she felt small and petite, and ridiculously horny.

"She's fine, Tom, it looks like our girl is fighting off the mating lust right now. You know, ice, there is no need to fight it. Tom and I will gladly help you scratch the itch you're feeling. You already know we want you." Bryson bent to speak against her neck and he pressed a soft kiss there before gently nipping at the skin. Her knees nearly buckled at the electricity that raced through her body, and her wolf howled with delight in her head.

A moment of indecision and a quiet tension filled the air, while she struggled with herself. Her body physically needed them, but her mind was fighting it every step of the way. The moment she gave into them, there would be no turning back. In fact, Thomas would be the one doing the turning, because he would be giving up his humanity to be her mate. There was just too much riding on it to make the decision while she was hungry, exhausted and worried about her parents.

"Thank you for the offer, Shakespeare, but I think I'll pass. Right now, all I can think about is food. Did you get extra cheese?" She pushed at Thomas's hands where they still gripped hers, and instead of letting her go, he pulled her with him as he moved back to the table. There was enough disappointment in his gaze to make her cringe with regret over her casual dismissal, but she needed a little more time to process this. Accepting her mates meant giving up her dream of time alone.

Pulling out a chair for her, Thomas handed her a napkin while she selected her slice of pizza. "I'm sorry I don't have anything more for you to wear, little one."

"It's okay, Devin said Rafe and his crew went on to Quiver Creek, while Ryley and the others searched for us. They should be here by morning. I can get some clothes from my bag then. Being a werewolf sure wreaks havoc on a girl's wardrobe."

Thomas and Bryson both chuckled, and KJ tried not to notice Bryson's still semi-hard erection tenting his pants, or the way Thomas's bare muscular chest flexed when he moved. No matter what her dreams *had* been, she knew there was no way she was going to be able to let these two go. Every moment she spent with them, they seemed to be wrapping themselves around her insides somehow. She was starting to understand the big bang everyone talked about with the mating lust. It just seemed to capture her mind, body, and soul, until separation was impossible.

"So, tell me, how do the other threesomes in your pack make it work?" Bryson asked as he took a seat on the nearest bed with a slice of pizza in his grip.

KJ looked at Thomas, who shrugged, and shoved pizza in his mouth. Rolling her eyes, she turned back to Bryson. "I've only known them for a little while. Rafe and Ryley are my brothers, my parents left them with the Gray Pack when they were kids while they went on the run from Nicolas. My understanding is that Caroline met Devin and Damon Gray, the pack Alphas, after her home caught fire. Devin and Damon are both firefighters who were called to fight the fire. They are identical twins, but they were pretty surprised to find out that they were sharing a mate. When my brothers met their mate, Shandi, they said that they never even second-guessed that she was going to be a shared mate. It was just how it worked. Are there no group matings at all in your pack?"

"Not that I've ever heard of. So, both of the other trios have pairs of siblings in them. It's really strange that you ended up with two strangers." Bryson gave Thomas a doubtful glance.

"I get it. You're freaked out by this whole thing, Bryson, so am I, but trust me when I tell you that Thomas is undoubtedly my wolf's mate too," she snapped at him, and he threw his hands up in a defensive gesture.

"Hey, I was just making a comment. Considering how easily I knew you were my other half; I can't doubt you. I'm just trying to adjust to the idea of sharing my mate with a guy I just met."

KJ stuffed a bite of pizza in her mouth and simmered on his words. Bryson was right. He and Thomas were strangers too. It had to be just as weird for the two of them. Hell, she hadn't even known Thomas for a full day yet, and she'd only spent the last couple hours with Bryson. Frustration filled her chest as she forced herself to eat the pizza. She could barely taste it going down, and the way her stomach was twisted in knots, she wasn't sure that it would stay down.

"Can we like, share bios or something? I would like to know a little more about the two people I'm going to have cubs and spend the rest of my days with," Bryson said as he accepted another slice of pizza from Thomas.

Thomas glanced at her, and when she shrugged this time, he gave her a small smile. "I'll start, I guess. You already know I'm a doctor. I've been working at a wound care clinic in Kansas City for the last couple years. When this trip came up, Tina and Devin thought that I might like to change careers and move into the den. I actually jumped at the chance. Believe it or not, it felt right. When we get back to the den, Tina and I are planning to open a medical clinic there, so the sick and injured pack members don't have to travel into town when they need help."

"Tina's your sister, right?"

"Yeah, she's actually a pediatric nurse, so it will work out great for us to open the clinic. Caroline Gray was an emergency room nurse, but she's pregnant with twins right now. Hopefully she will be able to help us out some, too, when the twins are older. Anyway, my parents are still living, and I hit the boxing ring to spar daily, other than that, I have spent most of my time working to pay off school loans. Your turn." Thomas gestured with another slice of pizza at KJ.

"Hi, I'm Katie Jo Whetstone, and I'm twenty-four—"

"Shit! You're only twenty-four?" Thomas interrupted, jumping out of his chair. "I'm eight years older than you are! Shit."

"Shut up and listen, old man, I want to hear her story," Bryson said with a laugh. KJ rolled her eyes at Thomas's dramatics.

"Age is just a number. I grew up everywhere, but mostly in Quiver Creek, Wyoming. My parents have told me for years that a bad man was after us and would kill me if he found me. They were right." She paused to take a deep breath and Thomas and Bryson both reached out and touched her to comfort her. "I got my diploma via home-schooling, but I've never been to college. I had this wild-ass dream of running away from everything after I got my parents settled in Kansas City, but it seems that fate isn't interested in my dreams. I found my two brothers when I reached K.C., only to have one of them call me a liar and vehemently deny our shared lineage. I spent a week listening to people try every possible way to counter my story, then I stumbled into my mate—who is not too old for me—but didn't exactly show up at the ideal time. Only to get wolf-napped, threatened, abused, and finally come face-to-face with a second mate that I'm not ready for. Now I'm sitting in a dirty motel room, wrapped in a towel, eating greasy pizza that will go directly to my already wide ass, and praying to God that my brothers get here before I do something I will regret because my inner wolf is having a hormone surge."

All the air expelled from her lungs in a huge whoosh when she finally finished, and she just sat staring at her pizza for a second, awaiting their response. When neither spoke, she finally looked up. Thomas and Bryson were both watching her intently with lust-dark-ened eyes again. A shiver ran down her back, and she tugged her towel tighter around her. This was getting damned uncomfortable. She wasn't going to be able to deny her physical need for the two men much longer.

"Little one, your ass is not wide, it's perfect, and I am dying to show you how much I like it," Thomas said, drawing her gaze to his melted-chocolate eyes. There was fire there, and the muscles of his neck and shoulders twitched as he fought to control himself.

Bryson moved to kneel in front of her. "KJ, I know we don't know each other yet, and we all had plans before this happened, but at least tell us you're willing to give this a chance."

His brilliant green gaze was hypnotic, and she nodded her agreement before she even realized she'd done it. The smile that spread across his face melted her heart, and she smiled back. He surprised her further when he brushed a soft sweet kiss over her lips, and then pulled back before she could beg for more. "Thank you. Are you done eating yet, peaches?"

"Yeah, I guess I wasn't as hungry as I thought," she said with a wide yawn. "That or finally getting all that off my chest was what I needed to rest."

"You crawl into the bed while Bryson and I clean up. We'll be there in a minute," Thomas said, cupping her chin in his hand while Bryson stood up.

"Both of you?" KJ squeaked, her eyes going wide. They were both going to get into the bed with her, touching her, close to her, and somehow she was supposed to resist them? How was that going to happen?

"Yes, both of us. If we're going to be mates, you're going to have to get comfortable with both of us. I don't know about Bry, but I'm a pretty affectionate guy, so I plan on holding you close every night from here on out. Nothing will happen if you don't want it to, little one," Thomas said, tossing their used napkins in the trash and meeting her gaze.

"Ditto that, Tom. I'll be the spoon from the backside. I can't wait to feel that lush ass against my…well, I guess I'll save that for another day. Into bed with you now, peaches." Bryson lifted the edge of the covers and helped her settle onto the bed. Just before he covered her up, he reached out and whipped off her towel, causing her to yelp in surprise. "No need for that shield, ice, no one here wants to hurt you."

He tucked the blanket up to her chin and bent to capture her lips. Instantly fire raced over her body and straight through to her clit. Her pussy moistened so much from kissing him that she was having a hard time thinking straight. His tongue pushed past her lips and stroked over hers, while his scent filled her nose and melted her control. Both of her hands went up to his shoulders and clutched at him. Desperately trying to push him away and drag him closer.

The need she felt growing in her stomach overwhelmed the fear she had been battling against, and she moaned into his mouth. If her lips had been free she might have begged him, but all she could do was grip him harder and press her chest up against his. The rough fabric of the motel bed sheet was abrasive on her nipples. All the sensations she was feeling were foreign to her, but she couldn't bring herself to be scared of what was happening. It was nature, and she wanted it to happen. More than she wanted to breathe, she wanted Bryson to make love to her at that moment.

When Bryson suddenly pulled back and broke their kiss, he stared down at her with lust-darkened eyes. "Yep. You are definitely my mate. I've never had a kiss like that in my life, love."

"That was fucking hot," Thomas said from a few feet away, reminding KJ that they weren't alone. She blushed, feeling ashamed at the blatant way she had rubbed against Bryson, like a bitch in heat. He must have noticed her withdrawal, because he was suddenly next to her on the bed, gripping her chin so she was forced to look him in the eye. "Don't do that! Don't turn away and refuse us. I wasn't lying, little one. Seeing Bryson kissing you was hot, and for whatever reason I'm not feeling even a bit of jealousy…Well maybe little, but only because it was his lips on you without mine on you, too."

Just like that Thomas swooped in for a kiss of his own and stole KJ's remaining ability to think or speak. She felt Bryson draw the covers down so her breasts were exposed, but she wasn't prepared when his mouth engulfed one of her hard nipples. A scream broke free from her voice box but was lost in Thomas's mouth. Having them both touching her was like dipping into a pool of lava. Her body was on fire, and she writhed underneath them, asking silently for release.

She could feel Bryson cupping her breast, as Thomas devoured her mouth, and she reached out to hold onto them. On one side her fingers tunneled into Bryson's hair, holding him close to her now swollen breast, while on the other side she cupped Thomas's jaw, running her finger over the whiskers that covered it.

Thomas broke the kiss, and stared down at her, "Little one, I want you, and I know Bry wants you, but it has to be your choice."

KJ looked to Bryson whose mouth hovered just millimeters from the peak of her nipple, watching and waiting for the go-ahead. They were giving her a chance to stop before it went too far. In that moment everything clicked in her brain, and even though she knew tomorrow she would feel regret over her lost freedom, she had to have the two of them.

"Yes, I want you both." She watched as the two men exchanged a glance, before nodding in silent agreement. As they simultaneously descended onto her aching body again, she let out a long moan of pleasure.

Thomas ran his tongue over her collarbone, while Bryson moved lower to her belly, and his tongue dipped into the recess of her navel. A bolt of lightning shot through her stomach the moment he tugged the rest of the blankets away from her nudity, and the cool air of the room hit her heated skin. Bryson continued to lavish openmouthed kisses over her hips and abdomen, but avoided that secret spot, as he made his way down her thigh to her knee and stroked the sensitive skin at the back.

Moisture pooled between her swollen pussy lips, and her hips rocked of their own accord, as Thomas gripped both of her breasts and squeezed them together, running his tongue over the twin crests teasingly.

"Please!" she whimpered, and clenched her eyes shut at the many sensations that were catapulting her closer to a level of intensity that she had never felt before.

"Shh...not so fast, peaches, we have plenty of time for fireworks, let's make this a slow buildup. Anticipation always makes it better," Bryson said against her ankle, right before he kissed the arch of her foot, making her toes curl.

She gasped, and her eyes shot open wide. "I wouldn't know! I've never done this before!"

Both men froze, and Bryson nearly dropped her foot from his grip. Thomas eased his hands away from her breasts and they stared at her in shock.

"What did you say, little one?" Thomas asked quietly.

KJ bit her lip and frowned suddenly feeling extremely vulnerable and exposed. Maybe she shouldn't have told them. Now that they knew she was a virgin they would probably never finish what they started. Her body was aching for some sort of release, and if they refused to give it to her, she might just lose her mind.

"Are you a virgin, peaches?" Bryson asked, his tone held a level of reverence that surprised her, and she nodded automatically.

"Fuck," Thomas said, and she dragged her eyes up to meet his. Instead of being angry, or judgmental, he looked pleased and even hornier than before. "I don't know how Bryson feels, but I'm honored that you would let me be part of your first time. I want you so much it's killing me, but if we need to stop right now, just give me the word."

KJ gave him a small smile before turning back to Bryson who still stared at her, looking rather shell shocked. "Bryson, I'm sorry, I should have told you before—"

He cut her off with a mind-numbing kiss, as he slid up between her thighs, pressing them wider with his hands. When they finally separated, they were both panting, and Thomas was grinning at them. "That is the sexiest thing I've ever heard, peaches."

"You guys aren't pissed?" she asked looking between the two of them. The way Thomas was licking his full lips, and Bryson's green eyes had darkened making her shiver. "Well then get on with it! Show me what I've been waiting for, boys!"

Their laughter was drowned out by her moans and soft growls, as Thomas kissed her senseless while pinching and pulling at her nipples, and Bryson started a slow descent back down her body to her dripping pussy. When he firmly put his hands on her inner thighs and forced them wide apart, she gasped and then squealed when his thumbs drew her puffy labia open to his view.

"Pretty in pink aren't you, peaches? You smell like candy," Bryson said just before he flicked his tongue into her folds.

She might have screamed, but she wasn't sure, in her head she could only hear the racing of her heart, and the rush of blood in her ears. The moment Bryson's tongue slid up to stroke over her tiny clit, she arched off the bed. Thomas pressed her back down, and moved from kissing her lips, to sucking at her nipples again. He alternated between her breasts, pinching one, then nipping the other, all while Bryson licked at her cunt.

A tsunami of sensation was building in her belly, and its center was between her quivering thighs. Bryson blew on her hot skin, and then chuckled when she growled at him. "That's it, peaches, come for me. Let me taste your sweet juice."

It broke over her, blocking out the rest of his words, and everything else that might have happened around her. All she knew was that her body exploded in an orgasm unlike anything she had ever been able to accomplish with her own fingers. Her pussy muscles clenched and unclenched inside of her so hard that she could feel her abs tightening with the motion. When she managed to pry her eyelids open again, it was to find Bryson with his chin resting on her pubic bone and her cream all over his lips, while Thomas sat above them, grinning at them both.

"Holy shit," she whispered.

"That was fucking incredible," Thomas said, and she giggled.

"You should have felt it from this end," she said playfully, and Bryson slapped her thigh gently.

"Oh, we will, love. No doubt about that!"

Bryson moved to tug his jeans off, exposing his thick, long erection to her curious gaze. For the first time since meeting him she let her eyes run over his form unabashedly. He was gorgeous, built of muscle and sinew, and rock hard from head to toe. Her fingers itched to run over every dip and curve, but more than anything she wanted to get her hand wrapped around the length of him.

The two men moved without any conversation, switching spots so Thomas was at the foot of the bed. He dropped to his knees and tugged her down until her butt rested on the edge of the mattress and her legs hung over his shoulders. Eyes level with her flooded cunt, he winked up at her. "My turn, little one. I'm going to stretch you a little before I take you, I don't want to hurt you."

She nodded, and then looked for Bryson. He was lounging next to her, with his body curved slightly around her head. His cock was within reach now, and she didn't hesitate to reach for him. "Whoa, getting brave now, peaches?"

His taunt hit its mark because she narrowed her eyes at him and tugged him closer. Just as she licked his tip, Thomas licked her pussy, and she jumped. "Easy! I don't want to lose a chunk of me because Tommy-boy is playing with your girlie bits!"

KJ started giggling, "Girlie bits?"

"Really, Bry? You have to make her laugh now? I didn't tell jokes while you were eating her pussy, did I?" Thomas said, his hot breath on her wetness making her shiver.

"Sorry man, but I have to protect myself."

KJ licked at Bryson's cockhead again. "I think I can handle it, but then again, I get lockjaw occasionally…"

The look on Bryson's face was priceless, and Thomas let out a loud laugh. "She's kidding, Bry! Now, fuck her face!"

KJ's stomach clenched at Thomas's dirty command. Did he realize how much his tone of voice turned her on? She wanted to do whatever would make him happy when he spoke like that, and she turned her attention back to the task at hand. Bryson's pre-cum was salty, and slightly musky, but it wasn't bad. She found herself going back to trace that little line around his head with her tongue. He seemed to be enjoying it, as he pressed his cock closer to her and threaded his fingers into her blonde hair.

"Suck on it, peaches. Gently, now…"

She took it into her mouth, carefully covering her teeth with her lips, and applied a little bit of suction. His growls of pleasure encouraged her to keep going, and she took it as far as possible, choking slightly when he pressed against her tonsils.

"Don't force it, love. Take what you can, but don't push yourself. Just having you touch me is good enough for me. Fuck that's beautiful." Bryson's head was thrown back, and his hips rocked gently as he did in fact fuck her face. It was empowering to realize that she could bring this enormous man to his knees with her mouth alone.

Thomas took that moment to slip his finger into her depths, and she gasped. The only fingers that had ever been inside of her were her own, and the feeling of being touched was more erotic than she could have fantasized.

"You like that, little one? Your greedy pussy is sucking my finger in, maybe you need more than one?" He pushed another finger into her tight passage, and she felt her body clamp down on him as she groaned around the mouthful of cock she had. If his fingers felt this magnificent how was it going to feel to be full of his cock?

CHAPTER SEVEN

*T*homas couldn't have pinpointed a more life changing moment, than the moment he rose to press his cockhead into KJ's warm, wet pussy. Her mouth was stretched around Bryson's cock, and her eyes were partially closed until her soft muscles began to stretch. He watched as her eyes widened, and she froze in her bobbing motion, her blue gaze darting to meet his. She released Bryson's cock and held her breath. Their eyes met, and held, as he slowly and gently pressed into her. The moment he reached the barrier of her virginity, he stopped, and pulled back a little, pressing forward again firmly. Her face tensed, and she whimpered as he pushed through her hymen, and claimed what nature had intended to be his all along.

Sinking all the way into her heat, he forced himself to stop and let her body adjust, fighting off the instinct to thrust into her roughly. She was too precious to use, and it meant more to him than he wanted to think about that she was allowing him to be her first. Watching her release Bryson's dick to focus on him sent a flutter into his already warm heart, and he smiled down at her.

"Slow and easy, little one. Tell me if I'm hurting you." With that, he began moving in and out of her, holding on precariously to the thin thread of control that he had left. When her hips began to rock up into him, he groaned, and dropped his gaze down to watch his own cock sliding into her pink folds. The golden curls that capped her mound were covered in her own juices, and her pussy lips eagerly gripped his swollen erection as he fed it into her.

He'd never experienced any sex that was more powerful than this. In fact, he wasn't sure that he would ever again experience a moment like this. His body and soul felt wrapped around the woman in his arms, and he wanted only to bring her pleasure.

"Thomas, please!" she whimpered, her fingers sliding up his arms to dig into his biceps, tugging him closer, and encouraging him to move faster. He picked up the pace, and when she began to pant and make sounds of approval in her throat, he pushed even deeper into her. When she tightened around him like a fist, he lost his hold on himself, and slammed into her, pouring cum deep into her womb, and dropping his chest to hers to take her mouth in a ravishing kiss. They were connected in more than just a physical sense. He could see the evidence of it in her pretty blue eyes when he broke their kiss and touched his forehead and nose to hers.

"Thank you, little one," he murmured to her, and she sighed heavily.

Her eyes shimmered with tears, and she gave him a small stunned half smile. "I never knew…Is it always like this?"

Thomas shook his head and pulled away from her. "No. I've never felt anything so intense. If I wasn't a believer in the mating lust before, I certainly am now."

He pressed one more kiss to her swollen lips, before meeting Bryson's gaze. Bryson had watched the whole thing, and Thomas was surprised that he hadn't minded. It had felt natural to have him there. There was no explanation for why he would be comfortable having sex in front of another man, but he wasn't going to argue it. Stretching out alongside KJ, he brushed the hair out of her face, and waited quietly for Bryson to make his move.

Bryson stared down at his mate. She looked well loved, and satisfied, at least until her blue eyes met his. Then somehow, they sparked with lust again. He had to admit, for just a moment he was afraid that she would only want Thomas, and after he took her virginity that she wouldn't want to make love again. His cock was pounding, and his balls were aching, as he waited for her to give him a sign. When she finally did, he sighed with relief.

Stretching out on his back, he wrapped his arm around her waist, and tugged her over on top of him.

"What are you doing, Bryson?" She giggled.

"Well, peaches, it's like this. I'm afraid that if I fuck you now, I won't be able to keep myself from biting you. So instead, you're going to fuck me. This way I can't reach your throat, and I can't lose control and claim you without you wanting me to," he explained, as he cupped her ass, and lifted her up over his hard cock.

"I–I–I'm not sure I can do this," she said, her eyes darting up to his hesitantly.

He gave her a reassuring grin. "If you can beg Tommy-boy to fuck you, then you can ride me like a cowgirl, peaches. Just do whatever feels good, trust me, I'll love it."

She quirked her eyebrow at his reminder of her wanton behavior, but otherwise she did as instructed, and slid her glorious pussy down over his erection, engulfing him in the fire that was her cunt.

Bryson heard a soft growl from her chest and watched the wonder on her beautiful face as she took in this new experience. Cupping her hips, he helped guide her in the rhythm, until she began thrusting her own body against his, and tossing her head back. Her long blonde hair was still damp from her shower, and it hung in ripples over her shoulders and back, flashing in the dim lighting of the motel room. He had never seen anything more beautiful, and his balls tightened.

Her full breasts bounced with her every movement, and he traced the curve of her hips with his hands, running them over every inch of skin he could reach. Her calves were tight against his outer thighs, and her fingernails raked down his chest and arms as she tried to grip him. His heart was stuck in his throat while he watched her, and he felt his canine teeth sink into his bottom lip. The tang of his own blood was on his tongue when her cunt tightened on him, and she began trembling.

Reaching up he pinched both of her nipples, arching his hips to meet her clit with his pubic bone. Her scream of pleasure shook him to the core, and he pumped his seed into her womb with a growl of his own. His wolf was howling with pleasure in his brain, and he bit his own lip trying desperately to maintain control. The need to claim her was so strong he wasn't sure he would be able to hold back when she slumped down on his chest leaving her neck dangerously close to his mouth.

Flipping their positions, he quickly pulled away from her, and walked on wobbly knees to the bathroom to clean up. His hands were shaking as he turned the cold water on in the shower. If that was vanilla sex with his mate, what was kinky sex going to be like? And how would he keep from hurting her when he finally did claim her? His mind was racing as emotions blasted him, and he gasped for air. The icy-cold water brought his raging temperature down, so he could think without his cock for a moment.

When he finally stepped out from under the water, he found Thomas standing in the doorway of the bathroom giving him a death glare.

"What?"

"What the fuck was that, man?" Thomas snapped at him, and Bryson frowned as he wrapped a towel around his waist.

"Sex? Haven't you had it before?" What was Thomas's problem? It was good for all three of them, and KJ was probably passed out on the bed sound asleep, right?

Thomas slammed his fist into Bryson's jaw, sending him backward a step. "What the hell?"

"You just rolled off her and left her, you dumbass. She thinks she did something wrong! What were you thinking?"

Bryson's heart stopped in his chest, and his stomach dropped to his feet. Pushing past Thomas, he turned the corner into the room to find KJ, curled up in the fetal position under the blanket, sobbing into the pillow. "Oh my God, peaches! I'm so sorry! I didn't—fuck—I mean —shit!"

Wrapping his arms around her stiff form, he forced her onto his lap, and buried his head into her neck, feeling like a complete asshole. "Stop, please, don't cry. KJ, I had to get away, or I was going to lose control. You didn't do anything wrong, baby! In fact, you did it so well, that I was losing my grip and had to get space so I didn't latch onto your throat before you gave me permission!"

Her sob caught in her throat, and she quieted in shock. Without even lifting her head she mumbled, "What?"

"My wolf was there, peaches. He was at the surface, and if I didn't get myself away from you, he was going to push me to claim you when you weren't ready. I won't force you like that. No matter what. I want it to be your choice always. I didn't mean to hurt you! I was trying *not* to hurt you!"

She pushed out of his lap, and stood there naked, with tearstains on her cheeks, and her fists on her hips. "You son of a bitch. I thought you were just being a jerk, and it turns out that you were trying to protect me? Why didn't you just talk to me? Maybe I wanted you to claim me. Did you ever think about that, Rambo?"

"Listen to yourself. You would have regretted it afterwards, and peaches, the last thing I want for us is for you to regret our mating. When you're ready for it, all you have to do is give me the go-ahead, and I will gladly make that dream reality, but I will always do every-thing in my power to protect you. Even if it means protecting you from yourself."

KJ threw a glance over her shoulder at Thomas, but the fury and hurt seemed to have deflated from her with his words. "I can't believe you wouldn't just talk to me. A word or two excusing yourself might have been nice."

"You're right. I'm a dumbass, but I'm a dumbass that's trying to be a nice guy," he said, running his hand through his blond hair in frustration.

The corner of her mouth lifted in a half smile. "Well, as long as we both agree on what a dumbass you were...I guess I can forgive you, but you better not ever pull a stunt like that again. Got it?"

He threw his hands up and grinned at her. "Scout's honor!"

"You aren't a boy scout!" Thomas said with a laugh.

"No, but I'll promise her the moon if she agrees to let me make love to her again," Bryson answered, as he snagged KJ around the waist and drug her back into his lap. "For the record, ice, you're damn hot when you're pissed off."

"I have a feeling you'll be seeing me that way a lot between the two of you," she said with a laugh.

As they settled into the bed, Bryson pulled her back flush against his front, and Thomas flipped the lamp off before climbing in and cuddling up to KJ's front. It didn't bother him when he felt his mate tangle one of her legs with Thomas's, and it didn't seem to matter to him that the knuckles of his hand were touching Thomas's ribs. What mattered was the fact that his cock was pressed into the crease of KJ's ass, and his hand was cupping her waist, holding her close. All the other details were trivial. After all, they were going to have to find a way to live together permanently, so touching was probably inevitable.

"Thank you for giving me another chance, peaches. I never want to hurt you," Bryson whispered against the nape of her neck. He nuzzled against that soft skin and kissed her gently.

"Mmm...thank you for being honest. If I had known that the sex was touching you as deeply as it was me, maybe I wouldn't have reacted so emotionally," she answered, shivering under his touch.

Thomas chuckled. "Something tells me that it won't be the only emotional outburst we have to deal with." A grunt of pain cut off anything else he might say, and Bryson assumed KJ had just elbowed him for the snarky comment.

"The only thing important to me now is keeping you safe and

happy, peaches. I know we have a learning curve ahead of us, but if you'll be patient with me, I'll do my best to make you happy."

She turned her head and pressed a kiss to his lips instead of answering him, and he fell asleep with a smile on his face. Maybe this mate thing wouldn't be so hard to get used to after all.

A hard knock on the door startled them all awake in the morning, and the two men both shot out of bed naked and tensed for attack. She relaxed when she heard the familiar voices of the other Gray Pack wolves talking just outside the motel room door. Why couldn't they have shown up in a few hours, after they all woke up and made love again. The fun was clearly over, and she was horny as hell. Who knew a pair of hot men could have her feeling this loose and easy?

Bryson's eyes widened and his nostrils flared as he picked up her arousal, but he just winked at her, and licked his lips. "We'll pick up where we left off later, love." His flaccid cock was thickening, and she couldn't tear her eyes away from it. "For now, it looks like the cavalry has arrived. Cover up those pretty titties, ice, unless you want your family to share in the view. They are a pretty shade of pink right now, and I remember how they taste like heaven."

KJ blushed, and threw a pillow at him, as Thomas pulled his pants on before heading to the door.

"Thomas? KJ? You guys in there?"

"Are you sure you got the right room, Ry?"

"Yes, I'm sure. Devin said it was room eighty-eight. Maybe they are sleeping?"

"Or maybe there should be a 'Do Not Disturb' sign on the door?"

KJ felt the heat climbing in her cheeks as she buried her face in her hands. This was the most humiliated she had ever been. Not only was her brother going to find her naked in a motel room with two men, but the smell of arousal and mating lust was so strong it would probably keep the other wolves standing outside the door for a while until it cleared.

Thomas jerked the door open, and a sound that was eerily similar to a growl rumbled from his chest as he glared unhappily at the three men on the other side of it. Noah grinned when he spotted KJ in the bed, but Cash and Ryley's attention was riveted on Bryson.

"Who the fuck are you?" Ryley asked, as Cash snarled. They were scenting Kaplan on Bryson, and if she didn't do something quick shit was going to hit the fan.

"Stop! Wait! Ry, this is Bryson, my mate." All eyes turned in her direction as she admitted the truth out loud. "Thomas and Bryson are *both* my mates."

Ryley's face went white, and Cash's broke into a wide grin. "Well doesn't that just beat all. You're mated to a Kaplan?"

Bryson nodded. "I was a Kaplan. Now my place in life is with her."

"Welcome to the family, man!" Cash said, stepping into the room and holding out his hand to Bryson. He drew up short and frowned at Thomas. "What do you think about it, Doc?"

Thomas sighed. "Well it's not like I got a whole lot of choice in the deal. I want the girl, and to keep the girl, I'll have to keep the pet—I mean Bryson."

Noah and Cash both laughed with Thomas, and Bryson even grinned, but Ryley stood frozen in the doorway. KJ moved over to him. "Ry? Are you okay? I know it's kind of sudden, but my wolf wants what she wants, right?"

Ryley reached out and hugged her close. "You're right. And as long as you're happy, I'm happy. Now, let's get you out of that sheet and into some clothes so we can hit the road. We haven't seen any sign of the Kaplans, but I don't doubt that they are close."

"Yeah, Nico will be furious that she's gone, and someone will have pointed out my absence by now," Bryson said, shaking Ryley's hand. KJ watched with amusement as the two men both gripped each other's hands tighter than was probably necessary and sized each other up. The testosterone was as thick in the air as the scent of sex.

"Have you heard from Rafe?" KJ asked anxiously.

Ryley nodded and frowned. "Yes, they got there late last night." When he didn't go any further, she growled at him. "It's not good, KJ. Rafe said she's really sick."

Her heart fell to her feet, but she swallowed hard against the tears that burned her eyeballs. "But she's still alive?" Bryson was at her side immediately, and she wondered if her emotions were somehow reaching out for him. She let him wrap his arms around her as she waited with bated breath for Ryley's next words.

"She was last night."

"Then get your asses moving, boys. I need to get home."

CHAPTER EIGHT

"She'll be all right, peaches. Stop worrying." Bryson's arm was wrapped around KJ's shoulder. Her head was pillowed against his chest, and her gorgeous blonde hair tickled his chin. Thomas sat on her other side with her hand cupped in his, and his fingers dancing over her palm. Neither man hesitated when she climbed into the van. They both followed and settled themselves around her like guard dogs.

Once they got dressed, and past the whole Kaplan lineage, Bryson had more time to survey KJ's older brother Ryley and the other two pack members present, cousins Cash and Noah Gray. Cash was a cowboy from head to toe, complete with a hat, large belt buckle in the shape of a wolf's head, and scuffed boots. Noah was younger than the others, closer to Bryson's age, with sandy brown hair, and lighter, hazel-colored eyes. He had a bulky build that was similar to Bryson's, and he seemed to be the most nonchalant about the situation. Ryley looked so similar to KJ that it was a little off-putting at first, but all three guys were easygoing once they knew that Bryson wasn't a threat, and he liked them instantly.

"Why do you call me that?" she asked without lifting her head.

"What? Peaches? Because your skin is the color of a ripe peach, and just about as soft. I've always loved peaches, and I'm already half in love with you." Bryson waited for her reaction and was relieved when she didn't argue. He knew she wasn't really ready to hear the words, but he wasn't going to lie to her.

"And you? You call me little one, why?" She directed this question to Thomas, and Bryson chuckled, answering for him.

"You really have to ask? Peaches you barely reach his chin in your bare feet. Seems like a no-brainer to me."

Thomas laughed, too, and smiled down at her. "He's right, but those aren't the words I would use. I see you as someone I want to protect, and care for. My own small piece of heaven. It would rip my heart out to lose you now, when I've just found you."

KJ contemplated Thomas's words for a few moments in silence, before responding. "You two do know you don't have to butter me up with sweet words to get into my pants, right?"

Both men burst out in laughter, drawing the attention of the other three guys who had been chatting in the front part of the van.

"What's so funny back there?" Ryley asked with a grin.

"Oh nothing, KJ is just setting the parameters for our relationship up front. Making sure we don't get the wrong idea about her," Thomas answered, lifting KJ's hand to his lips.

"Good. If she can't enforce those rules, I'll help her out," Ryley said with a wink at them all to let them know he was teasing.

Bryson let himself sink back into the seat, feeling more relaxed and carefree than he had in years. These people were nothing like the Kaplan Pack wolves, and he was relieved to find that he wanted to be a part of them. The sense of camaraderie and familial bond was nice.

"You never got around to giving us your bio, Rambo," KJ said, shifting so she was looking up at him, and he couldn't resist pressing a quick kiss on her soft lips.

Her sigh of pleasure sent a wave of warmth through his chest, and he nuzzled her temple while he began to speak. "I guess we did get interrupted, didn't we. Okay, well, I'm twenty-six, and I was born into the Kaplan Pack, if you haven't already guessed. I have only been in Nico's crew of Omegas for about three months, before that I was a regular guard for the pack back home in Alaska. When the opportunity to head south came up, I jumped on it. I've never really liked the cold weather or the long, deep dark of winter back home. My parents are still alive, but they are loyal to their Alpha, so we aren't close. They don't like hearing me talk badly about how the pack is run. I also have a pair of younger twin brothers, Ryan and Adam. They are only a year younger than I am, and they left the den to go to Anchorage for school. They both agreed with my views on the pack, but they chose to look for a way out of it. In fact a lot of wolves are leaving the Kaplan family lately."

"Why?" Cash and Noah were both turned around to face him, while Ryley kept watch in the rearview mirror.

Bryson shrugged. "Evan Kaplan is a terrible Alpha. He tends to let Nicolas run things, while he indulges himself with a variety of women and other vices, spending pack money on his own personal desires. Nicolas is a strong leader, but he's a mean bastard, so when he is back home at the den, everyone avoids him like the plague. Things are the calmest when he's gone, but there is also no form of leadership."

"So on good days a militant rogue with a grudge is leading the pack, and on bad days a male chauvinist with an addiction problem is? Sounds like a blast, my friend," Cash said with a hollow laugh.

"What did you do for Nicolas?" KJ asked, frowning.

"Mostly patrols, but recently we had started stepping it up around Quiver Creek. Before this assignment I had been part of the security detail that dealt with problem wolves and humans."

"Problem wolves?" Cash asked the question they were all thinking, and all eyes were on Bryson expectantly waiting for an explanation.

"Yep. Any wolf or human that disagreed with the Kaplans was banished from the pack or gotten rid of." Bryson felt the guilt creeping up his throat, but KJ's eyes held no judgment.

"Have you ever killed someone for them?" she asked softly, and he hesitated. Part of him wanted to lie to her so the she wouldn't know the details that sometimes woke him up at night, but it was impossible.

"Yes. It was my job, and I was good at it," he said, trying to keep his expression bland. Her slow perusal of him had him fidgeting, and when she finally nodded her acceptance, all the tension dissolved from his body. At least she wasn't going to release him because of his past. Maybe they did stand a chance.

"Do you know why Nicolas had KJ kidnapped?" Noah asked.

"All I know is that we had orders to bring her in alive. Finding her with a human was a bit of a shock. I was at our temporary camp when they brought the two of them in, and the moment I realized she was my mate I started working out a plan to get her out of there. I hadn't planned on a stowaway, but since she likes him, I brought him along." Thomas rolled his eyes, and Bryson grinned. Maybe having Tom as a partner wasn't going to be as bad as he first thought. Just the mental images from last night were burned into his brain. Remembering had Bryson's cock thickening behind his jeans, and he shifted to alleviate the pressure.

"Kaplan said that there was gold left by my grandfather. He wanted that, and he said he was going to make me his sex slave because Mom was too old for his taste now."

"Oh that's just sick," Cash said looking pale faced.

Thomas and Bryson exchanged a look over KJ's head. "It's not going to happen, little one. We're going to protect you. Now that we know that Nicolas is close by looking for you we'll be even more cautious. How far out are we from Quiver Creek, Ryley?"

"Less than a half an hour now. Did anyone call Devin to let them know we picked you guys up safely?" Ryley asked.

"I'm on it now," Cash said, pulling his cell phone from his pocket. After a moment he spoke. "Damon? Yeah, hi, it's Cash. We have the packages safely in our possession…Yeah, both of them, and their mate." Cash chuckled at whatever Damon said back and glanced up to smile at the three of them cuddled together in the back seat. "Yeah, it seems that one of the Kaplan wolves and Thomas are both meant to be mated to KJ. Weird I know, but what can you do? We're about a half an hour away now…Yeah, have you heard from Rafe's crew? Good, we'll see them when we get there then…Did the Diego Pack get to the den? What? Are you serious? Holy shit!"

Cash's eyes shot to Ryley, and he looked stunned as he sat silently on the phone listening to what Damon was saying. He swallowed hard, and everyone tensed while they waited to find out what was happening back home. "Yeah, okay, well I'll tell Rafe and Ryley, but don't be shocked if they go ape shit and head for home immediately. Okay, we'll see you guys soon. Bye."

"Tell me what? What the hell is going on?" Ryley demanded. His blue eyes were hard and looked terrified. "Is Shandi okay?"

Cash held up his hands. "Shandi is fine! You can call her when we get to Quiver Creek to verify that. But Whitney seems to have found herself a pair of mates too."

"What?" Noah, Thomas, and KJ all said at the same time. Bryson just watched the drama unfolding before him.

"Who is Whitney?" he whispered loudly to KJ.

"My little sister!" Ryley snarled, and Bryson frowned in confusion. "My adopted little sister. Cash, you better keep talking."

"It seems that when the Diego Pack arrived at the den, our little Whitney came face-to-face with her own mates. Cadence Diego being one of them," Cash said.

"You have got to be fucking kidding me," Noah said with a wide, shit-eating grin on his face. Ryley's golden skin darkened with anger, and he glared at the road ahead of him, clenching his jaw.

"What is up with you Gray wolves and having multiple mates? Are your women that difficult that they need two men?" Bryson asked, and then yelped when KJ's elbow found his kidney.

"Ry, you can't stop it from happening, so just breathe through it. Whitney is a strong enough woman to handle an Alpha wolf as her mate. She will be fine," Cash said calmly.

"So the Alpha challenge is done?" Noah asked.

Cash shook his head. "No, but there are only a few contenders, and my understanding is that Cadence has it in the bag. Whitney was born to be an Alpha Bitch. I have no doubt she'll be okay."

"I'll call the den as soon as we get safely parked. I need to hear that from her," Ryley said quietly, still looking like he wanted to rip something apart with his teeth.

"Why are the Diego Pack wolves having their Alpha challenge with you guys?" Bryson asked. Suddenly he was feeling very left out of the group, as he didn't understand completely what was going on.

"The Diego Pack Alpha, Barton Diego, was killed when he attacked our Alpha Bitch, Caroline. He kidnapped her and Tina, Liam's mate, and was going to kill them. Cadence Diego is his son, and next in line for being Alpha of the pack. Because he felt bad about Barton going psycho, Devin offered to host the Alpha challenge at the Gray Pack den. It will ensure that it's fair."

"So is Cadence Diego anything like his daddy?" Bryson asked, and then wished he would have kept his trap shut as Ryley growled from the front.

"He better not be."

KJ sat between her two mates feeling anxious and horny, and trying her damnedest to stay focused on the conversation around her. Bryson's arm encircled her, making her feel secure and warm, but the T-shirt plastered to his broad chest was thin enough that she could feel his muscles flexing whenever he spoke or laughed. It was torture to not be able to crawl into his lap, and seat herself on his still semi-hard cock. Her eyes kept drifting to the zipper of his jeans where she could clearly see that the bulge remained. When he caught her looking, he just smirked and winked.

Then there was Thomas, her human. His scent was very different from Bryson's but the two combined made her feel like she was losing her mind. Every now and then he would turn those chocolate eyes her way and look at her with such care and concern that she wanted to throw herself into his arms and never come out. He seemed to enjoy taking care of her, and as much as she liked her independence, being doted on was kind of nice.

Thomas was currently drawing lazy figure eights on her palm with the tip of his finger. Every stroke over her skin sent a ripple of heat through her body straight to her clit. She glanced up to find his smoldering gaze on her, and his full lips quirked up in a grin. She loved that look on his face already, and it irritated the human side of her. So much for exploring her freedom and sowing her wild oats. Once she had assured herself of her family's safety and clarified plans to load the pack up for Kansas City, she planned on locking Thomas and Bryson in a room with her until the mating lust was sated. Her wolf needed them, and if she was honest, her heart was already involved. *Fuck a duck*, she thought to herself, *I can't believe I'm one of those women who falls so easily.*

A moment later, she caught the scent of home on the air, and she squealed, releasing Thomas's hand, and pulling away from Bryson. "Home!"

"Wait a sec, KJ, we're almost there, sit still." Thomas—ever the reasonable one—was trying to pull her back in her seat, but her need to see her family had her wolf busting at the seams.

Ripping away from him, she squeezed through the narrow gap between the bench seat and door and threw the lever to open it. The van was slowing, and she could hear everyone yelling at her, but she could also feel her body shifting. Its truest nature coming to the surface and all her fears, sadness, and the exhaustion of her long journey were melting her control. She leapt from the moving van into the grass at the side of the road and shifted before her feet even touched down. Her clothes ripped away from her, and she had a momentary thought of how limited her wardrobe was getting to be, before she scented her family again on the breeze. Like that, all her other thoughts were gone, and she was racing through the trees around the bend and into the clearing she had called home for the last decade or so.

Just like always, the pine trees soared into the blue sky and the mountains curved around their little clearing, leaving only room for a few cabins, a storage building, and a meeting hall. All were crudely built, but they represented home to her. She was brought up short as the pungent scent of smoke hit her wolf, and she took in the missing homes around her.

Her place of security and comfort was a ravaged shell of war. The Griffin cabin was completely gone, only the stone chimney remained in the midst of the charred earth. Nearby, there were only remnants left of Wesley and Zara Todd's cabin. What had happened here?

Warmth at her side, and the scent of Bryson and Cash drew her attention and she glanced at the two wolves before turning back to the devastation. She was grateful for their presence as she slowly made her way closer to the camp. A roaring sound in her ears blocked out any voices, as she struggled to keep her emotions under control, but a flash of movement and then the sight of her father in human form walking toward her with Rafe and Owen sent her running in his direction. She shifted just before she jumped into her father's arms and wrapped her own tightly around his neck.

"Daddy! What happened?" Tears were falling down her cheeks unchecked, and she took deep gulping breaths just to get his scent back in her brain.

"It's okay, Katie-baby. We had a little rough patch with the Kaplan wolves last night, but now that you brought your brothers here, we're going to be okay. I'm so proud of you, baby!"

Ryley parked the van just as Thomas caught sight of a naked KJ fly into the arms of a tall blond man. Jealousy balled in his gut, until he saw Rafe and Owen right behind the man. The way the guy held KJ told him that this had to be her father, Graham Whetstone. Moving a little slower just because his nerves were jangling, he made his way from the van over to the small group with Ryley and Noah at his side.

Bryson and Cash were standing naked next to Rafe and Owen,

and Thomas marveled at how comfortable everyone seemed with their nudity. He wasn't thrilled that his woman was standing here in the buff for the whole world to see, but clearly, he was the only one with an issue.

When KJ finally released her father and turned around, she sought him out with her eyes and his jealousy was soothed. Even with tears on her cheeks and worry in the blue depths of her eyes, she was the most beautiful woman he had ever seen. Without thinking about his surroundings, he stepped to her side, and tugged her into his arms, kissing her temple as he wrapped his arms protectively around her. If she was hurting, then he was going to do his damnedest to make things right for her.

Bryson seemed to feel the same need to hold her close, as he moved to them and pressed against KJ's back, nuzzling her neck, and gripping her hips. A chuckle and a growl drew all them back to the present, and Thomas looked up to find all eyes on them.

"So I heard that you found your mates, Katie-baby. I sure hope these two are the right wolves, because otherwise they are dead men walking," Graham teased, and Thomas glanced down at KJ worriedly.

She rolled her eyes at her dad and smiled back at Thomas. "Yep, Dad, this is Doc and Rambo, otherwise known as Thomas Jameson, and Bryson Samuels."

Graham shook Bryson's hand first, albeit warily. "You're a Kaplan."

Thomas saw Bryson flinch, but he held Graham's gaze. "Yes, sir, I was born a Kaplan. However, I've severed my ties with the pack now that I've found my mate—your daughter."

Graham grunted as if to say, "yeah right" and faced Bryson head-on. "Really? So if your pack mates attack us again...would you kill them to protect her?"

There was no hesitation in Bryson's words, and they echoed the thoughts in Thomas's head. "Sir, I would kill for her, and I would die to protect her."

Graham nodded after a moment, and seemed to accept Bryson's

proclamation, as he turned to shake Thomas's hand. "Jameson? You're the human doctor the guys were telling me about. Thank you for coming. I hope you're able to help Tasha, but…well, we'll get to that in a minute." Graham glanced over at his daughter and lifted an eyebrow. "Why am I not surprised that you ended up with two mates, Katie-baby?"

"Well it wasn't my idea!" she said with a frown. "I didn't even want *one* mate!"

Thomas heard Bryson growl low in his throat, and he wished he could do the same. It didn't sit well with him when KJ started talking about how she didn't really want the future that she had now.

"Do you want to tell me why one of your mates is still human, and why you don't have mating marks just yet? My understanding is you three spent the night together."

"KJ wasn't expecting to find her mates yet, and Bryson and I didn't want her to feel forced into making a decision while she was so emotional. It was important to complete our mission first," Thomas answered.

The answer seemed to please all the wolves present, and the subject was dropped. Everyone's attention was diverted as an older woman with long blonde hair the color of wheat appeared on the path. Her movements were slow and unsteady, and her skin tone was a sickly gray color. The medical practitioner inside of him blasted to the front, and he let go of KJ to move to the woman's side. His hands went to her arm, acting as support as she moved closer. She was clearly very ill. When the woman turned two clear blue eyes up to meet his gaze, he realized this was KJ's mother, Tasha.

"Ma'am, you need to be resting. You don't look well." He stood as still as possible, while she gripped his arm to hold herself steady.

"Thank you, but I'll be all right. I had to come see my baby."

"Mama!" KJ ran into Tasha's arms, and the two women clung to each other for several moments, tears blending together.

"KJ, your mate is right, we need to get your mama back into the cabin and in bed. That way Doc can check her out," Graham said, moving forward to take Thomas's place next to Tasha.

"Oh hush, you didn't think my girl was going to arrive without me greeting her, did you? And to finally see my baby boy again…" Tasha looked up at Ryley who looked like he had just seen a ghost. "Ryley?"

CHAPTER NINE

*Y*esterday when Rafe stepped out of the van and stood before a man who could be no one but his father, the air vanished from his lungs and his mouth dried up. His own blue eyes stared back at him, and even his eyebrow had the same arrogant arch. It was uncanny. Today he was face-to-face with his biological mother and father, as well as his younger brother who had turned a sickly shade of green.

He had been delaying asking the questions his heart ached to have the answers to, until Ryley was there. The pending conversation was absolutely necessary, but at this moment he wished that he was anywhere but here. He needed answers, and the only way to get them was to sit down and listen with an open mind.

How am I supposed to be open-minded to the two people who tore my heart out when I was just a kid?

Anger bubbled and churned in his gut as they all entered the Whetstone's cabin. The living room was small, made smaller by the crowd of werewolves who settled themselves around it patiently waiting for the fireworks to start. A sofa, two chairs, an ottoman, and a window seat were filled to capacity, leaving just the dining set for Rafe,

Ryley, KJ, and their parents. Bryson and Thomas hovered close to KJ, refusing to leave her even to sit across the room.

As he took his seat, Rafe stared down at the scarred wooden table-top, seeing himself in it. He had only recently realized that happiness was possible after meeting his new wife Shandi, and yet here he sat just days after his wedding, with strangers in a strange place. His heart and soul were bruised, and scarred, just like the oak under his fingertips, but just beneath that mottled surface he could see the strength, and resilience of the solid piece of furniture. He hoped that he would be as resilient after hearing what his parents had to say to him, because right now he felt pretty weak.

In a moment of shameless emotion, he had hugged his mother when he came face-to-face with her after so many years, weeping on her shoulder like the child he was when he'd last seen her. She cried and held him, rocking with the intensity, but neither spoke of their pain, or questioned their anger. Now she faced him head-on. Her chin was tilted defiantly, and her blue-green eyes were steady even as pain etched deep grooves into the skin around them. When she lifted her hand to place it in her husband's, Rafe could see it trembling though he didn't know if it was from the weakness in her body, or the emotional situation.

His eyes jumped from Tasha to Graham to KJ to Ryley in quick succession, unable to settle and express what he needed to get off his chest. Ryley didn't seem to have such problems.

"Well, this is not exactly the family reunion I had always hoped for," Ryley cracked, sending a nervous chuckle through the other Gray wolves around the room.

Tasha smiled wistfully at her younger son. "No, it's certainly not what your father and I had hoped for when we first left the Gray Pack den all those years ago."

"But you still left," Rafe snapped a little too harshly, drawing a hiss of irritation from KJ.

Tasha flinched, but turned to hold his gaze. "Yes, we did. Rafe, I can see you're full of anger, and for that I'm so sorry. I wanted to be the mother you needed, holding your hand as you walked to school, reading you stories at night as I tucked you into bed, watching you grow and change…but that wasn't possible. Nicolas Kaplan wouldn't have left us alone."

Rafe held his tongue for a moment, thinking through her words, and biting back the tears that burned his eyes. "I've heard that part from KJ, but what I want to know, is why you didn't want us with you when you ran? You can't say it was too dangerous, because you took KJ with you when you had her."

Graham shook his head, "Son, it was too dangerous. Nicolas had already threatened to take the two of you away from us if he caught us. He said that he would torture Tasha with her own children if she didn't fall into line. He's a nasty person, Rafe, and we could only imagine what he would have done to two small boys to get your mother to do what he wanted."

"And KJ? She wasn't worth protecting?"

"KJ came a couple years later, after we'd managed to lose Nicolas for a little while. Graham wanted to go back to get you boys, but I wouldn't let him. I couldn't tear you away from the only life you had known, and the happy family that you had built with Henley and Victoria. Not for my own selfish need to have you with me. I knew that Nicolas wasn't done with us, but I couldn't bring myself to let go of another child. The most selfish thing I've ever done was keep Katie Jo with us. I should have let your father take her to Victoria too, so she could be raised with you two."

"What? Mama, why would you say that?" KJ's face was a pale gray color and her mouth dropped open as tears started to fill her eyes.

"Because, my love, you have grown up to be resentful of your own family. You have spent your whole life hiding and running and avoiding the world, and it's because I was too scared to face-off with Nicolas Kaplan. I'm sorry for that." Graham moved to wrap his arm around Tasha as tears slipped down her pale cheeks to match her daughter's.

Rafe watched as KJ began to shake with the release of emotion, and Thomas lifted her into his arms, settling into the chair with her cradled in his lap. Bryson's hand found her shoulder, and he rubbed small circles against her skin, trying his best to soothe her. Rafe couldn't help feeling a wave of acceptance for the two men. They were silent, but supportive, which was just what was needed. Homesickness and longing for his own mate curdled his stomach further, and he realized he was grinding his teeth.

"So what now? You want us to just forgive and forget, and you come live with us in Kansas City like nothing ever happened?"

Graham growled at his oldest son's anger, but Tasha stayed him with a pat on the hand. "He's right, Graham. We can't just pretend this didn't all happen. I had hoped you would be able to forgive us when you heard the truth, Rafe, but I understand if you can't." She paused and leaned into her husband. "The truth is, children, that I'm dying. I can feel it, and I have known it ever since the moment I was shot. The bullet was silver, and it is poisoning me slowly. I can't eat anymore because I can't keep anything down. My blood pressure has dropped, and my body is growing weak."

"No, Mama! We brought Doc so he could get the bullet out. You'll be fine after he does that!" KJ's voice was high-pitched and panicky.

"I'm sorry, my love. I am so thankful that you were able to find him, and your other mate, and I appreciate the thought, but even if the bullet comes out the damage is done," Tasha said sadly.

"With all due respect, Mrs. Whetstone, it doesn't hurt to try. There is no excuse for a person to give in to death when you have so much to fight for," Thomas said, and Rafe felt even more pride for this strong man that would care for his little sister.

"I didn't say I wouldn't try, but I need Katie Jo and her brothers to accept the inevitable and move beyond grieving. It is important that everyone be moved to the Gray Pack den as quickly as possible. I'm afraid that Nicolas is regrouping for another attack like the one Rafe, Owen, and Luke came upon last night. Our numbers are too small to continue to fight like this."

Rafe looked to the silently brooding Ryley and sent his thoughts at his brother.

Well? What now?

I thought that we would have some sort of family after they came back, but now...well look at her, man! She looks like she's dying.

I think she's right, but I don't want to push KJ. She's been through a lot.

Wow! That's something I never thought I'd see!

What's that?

You protecting your little sister!

Shut up, asshat.

"Stop it, boys," Graham said loudly, and both brothers turned matching looks of shock on him. He just laughed at them both and shook his head. "No, I can't hear you, but I've been around enough sets of siblings to know when you're having a silent conversation."

The brothers breathed a sigh of relief, but the tension remained high in the air.

"I think I need to lie down for a little while. KJ, love, will you help me to the bedroom?" Tasha looked as if she had aged a decade in just the few moments they had been talking, and Rafe watched as KJ jumped from Thomas's lap and helped her stand. Thomas rose too and followed the two women into the bedroom after exchanging a silent look with Bryson. When the bedroom door clicked closed, Graham dropped his head into his hands, and let out a long shuddering breath.

Rafe couldn't find the right words to comfort him. As much as he hated seeing someone hurt, he wasn't yet sure of Graham's place in his life. He had a father. Henley Gray had been the man who taught him to throw the perfect spiral pass on the football field, and how to track other animals in the woods, and he stood beside him on his wedding day. Graham Whetstone had barely been a blip in the life he remembered, so why did his heart ache to hug the man and ask for his approval? Nothing seemed to make sense in his world anymore.

I need to talk to Shandi, she will help me put it all into perspective again. With that thought in his brain he stood and moved toward the front door. "Ryley, I'm calling home if you would like to join me."

Ryley was on his feet and moving to his side before he finished the words. Graham stopped them both as they opened the door. "Boys, thank you for at least hearing us out. I know we made a mistake, and I also know we can't go back in time to fix it, but I hope that somehow, some way, you will find it in your heart to forgive her before she dies. Let us go in peace."

The cold reminder of Graham's fate hit Rafe like a sucker punch. Werewolves couldn't survive without their mate after bonding. In a triad, two of the three could continue, but in a pairing when one died, the other would shortly follow. It was something about the mating bond that caused them to just wither away. If Tasha was right, and she was facing the end, then it meant that Graham, who was otherwise healthy, was also facing death. What a clusterfuck this trip had turned out to be.

KJ and the others waited in the living room of the Whetstone cabin, while Thomas took care of her mother's wound in the master bedroom. Rafe and Ryley had just gotten off the phone with their mate, Shandi, and they both looked homesick and shell-shocked. After settling her mother into Thomas's care with Graham at her bedside, KJ had immediately moved to introduce her Quiver Creek family to her new Gray Pack family. The room seemed even more crowded as they all came together to discuss the attack that Rafe, Luke, and Owen came upon the night before.

"What happened here, Rudy?" She looked to her parents' oldest and dearest friend and waited while he tried to find the right words. She could almost see his brain working. "Don't do that! Please, just tell me the truth."

"Yesterday the Kaplan wolves attacked the den in the middle of the night. They didn't bother with trying to fight us, instead they just threw lit torches of some sort into the windows of various cabins on the outer edges of the den. I suppose they were trying to run us out. Anyway, instead of running for the woods, we banded together and managed to save a couple the cabins with water from the creek. I just wish we had been able to save more. Rafe and the boys got here and were able to help us run them off before they did more damage." He looked sadly over at Kayla Griffin who held her sleeping young daughter Mari. The Griffins were one of the families who lost their home in the fire, and now had to start over.

"Unprovoked?" Cash asked, and Rudy turned angry eyes on the cowboy.

"Of course, it was unprovoked! What do you think we did, stand out there waving a red flag and yelling come get me? We might not be big city, but we aren't stupid."

"Easy there, big guy. I didn't mean to upset you. I'm just trying to get all the facts straight so when one of those Kaplan dogs gets close enough, I can tell him why I'm ripping his throat out and watching him bleed to death." Cash's vehemence drew a startled gasp from Kayla, and he grimaced and touched his cowboy hat. "Pardon. Sometimes my mouth runs away with me."

Kayla was one of the many women who couldn't seem to resist Cash's good ol' boy act, and she smiled back at him. "If it were about anyone but those Kaplan wolves I would be offended, but I say, go get 'em."

Cash laughed along with everyone else, and KJ turned back to Rudy. "So what now?"

Rafe cleared his throat. "Once we know more about your…I mean…Mom's health we'll determine how fast we can pack up and hit the road. No matter what we have to drive straight through, the Kaplans have already proven that they are tracking us and waiting for us to slip up."

KJ felt the blood drain from her face. "Rudy, did you know that Nicolas Kaplan had his sights set on me and not Mom?"

Rudy's dark eyes locked on her face but didn't reveal anything. He nodded slowly, and all the air in KJ's lungs hissed out.

"Why didn't you tell me? When did he stop tracking Mom and choose me as his target?"

"Didn't change anything. The whole time we were protecting Tasha, we were also protecting you. That's just the way it is. Who cares what his goal was, as long as he didn't achieve it, we're doing our jobs."

KJ huffed in frustration, but Bryson's hand on her shoulder had her biting back a smart-ass reply. She looked back at him as he ran his hand over her hair gently, soothingly. His presence was comforting, but kept her libido on edge, too.

"Rudy, what do you know about the gold?" Bryson asked, and suddenly KJ felt the air in the room turn ice cold. All the Quiver Creek wolves tensed and glared at Bryson.

Kayla's husband Samson spun to face Bryson with anger and suspicion in his eyes. "Why? You planning on running back to your pack and sharing information?" Samson was an enormous wolf. He stood nearly seven feet tall, with short blond hair, and hard gray eyes. He carried a scar on the lower part of his jaw, but if asked about it he would only say that it was from his past life. He and Kayla had four daughters, Lily, Daisy, Rose, and Mari, who ranged in age from twenty-six to their surprising youngest who was just seven. They had been a part of the Quiver Creek Pack for a long time, and their daughter Lily was KJ's only female friend. Samson was particularly protective of KJ.

Bryson's green eyes flashed with irritation, and he growled. "Back off, wolf. I'm here for my mate, where she is, I am, and no more than that. I won't betray you, if you don't betray me. That way neither of us has to die."

Samson eased back and gave Bryson a once-over. Turning to KJ he gave her a weak smile. "I might actually like this one, Katie Jo. He has some backbone."

"Thanks. I think. Rudy, what do you know about the gold?" KJ said, gritting her teeth.

"I only know the story secondhand from your mama, so don't expect the details. Your grandpa, Joe Raullins, had a gold claim up in the Klondike. He hit it big more than fifty years ago, but he shut down the mine shortly after he struck gold. Tasha said that he never wanted to be wealthy, and that he believed the gold brought a curse on him. To the best of my knowledge he still owns it, and it's still full of gold, but no one knows where it is, except for Joe."

There was silence in the room for a moment before KJ asked, "Are you telling me that he had a fortune at his fingertips, and he didn't mine it?"

Rudy nodded, and frowned. "That's what I know. I'm sorry I can't be more help."

"Well it does explain why Nico wants KJ. The pack has been really struggling for funds for the last fifteen years or so. Evan Kaplan spends the money faster than we can bring it in. I have a feeling that Nico intends on challenging his cousin for the Alpha position, and if he has that gold he will have the pack's support," Bryson said, and KJ looked up into his worried eyes.

"Good thing I have you and Doc to protect me now, huh?" KJ winked up at him, hoping to ease his stress, but her own nerves were jangled. Why had her mother never shared any of that information with her? A spark of illogical jealousy flamed to life in her chest, and tears burned her eyes as she shifted to lean into Bryson. He accepted her easily, holding her gently against his strong chest. Maybe having a mate wasn't going to be so bad.

At that moment Graham and Thomas stepped back into the room, pulling the bedroom door shut behind them. Graham looked lost and scared, and KJ jumped up to run into his arms and hug him tight.

Thomas watched them hold each other for a moment, and then turned back to the group. "Anyone got anything to drink around here? Something strong?"

Samson nodded to Brick Poplin who headed into the kitchen to retrieve the requested drink, and then asked the question they all shared, "How is she, Doc?"

Thomas grimaced, and his eyes flicked to KJ. "I'm sorry, but she's not good. The bullet is definitely silver, and it's embedded deep. There is so much infection now, that I'm concerned that even getting it out of her won't allow her to heal."

"So we just let her die?" KJ asked sounding panicky.

"I want to get her to a hospital where they can do surgery to remove the bullet and irrigate the wound," Thomas said with a heavy sigh as he took the glass of amber liquid that Brick handed to him.

"We can't take her to a human hospital here, we don't have any doctors that know our secret, and if it gets out…well I don't need to tell you the risk that would be," Graham said with a shake of his head. "There has to be something else we can do."

"Then we have to get her back to Kansas City as fast as humanly…I mean as fast as possible. I can't do surgery alone, but Tina and Caroline could help me. Getting that bullet out of her body is the only chance she has," Thomas said. He turned and faced KJ and Graham, staring into KJ's eyes. "To be honest, I'm not sure that I can save her. Like she said, she may be too far gone."

Suddenly, KJ couldn't see anything, the blackness that had been threatening to consume her finally did, and she felt herself falling. Her last thought was that it was damn unlucky to gain two brothers and two mates in the last two weeks only to have to give up her mother and father.

CHAPTER TEN

*B*ryson's heart jumped in his chest when he saw KJ's eyes roll up into her head and her knees buckle. Graham was able to catch her before she hit the floor, but the image would be burned into Bryson's brain forever. There was no way he could ease the fear and pain she was feeling, and as he watched Thomas take KJ from Graham, he ached for him as well. Thomas was dealing with more guilt and pressure than anyone should have to handle.

"Rudy has cleared his cabin so you three can stay there. Take her now, and let her rest for a while. But you two need to bond with her before something else happens. In your human form you're the weakest link we have, Doc, but Rafe tells me that once you mate with my Katie-baby you will shift. I appreciate that you want to protect her, but at this point you're no match for the wolves that are attacking us." Graham's words struck Thomas, and his face went pale, making the dark color of his facial hair even darker.

Bryson's heart twisted for his new partner. Here was a man who just weeks ago was living a normal human life, and now he was bound to be turned into a werewolf and face the fire of battle alongside the rest of a pack of strangers. Could this get any stranger?

They followed Rudy out of the cabin and down the central path of the den. The cabins were set up in a circular layout of sorts, with the Whetstone cabin and the meeting hall being in the very middle, and then other cabins feeding out from them. Sort of like the spokes on a wheel, with one main path connecting them all to each other.

"I won't force her," Thomas said softly as they walked. The old man limped on cane, and his back was bent, his hands gnarled. He looked as ancient as KJ had described him, but his mind seemed to be as sharp as a tack.

"You won't have to, son. The mating lust is very strong between the three of you, and she's already carrying your scent. It's light, but I can smell it on her. All you have to do is be there for her. Her wolf is likely to do the rest." Rudy paused when they reached the porch steps of his cabin and sniffed the air. His dark gaze searched the area around them, and Bryson went on alert.

"What is it?"

Rudy shook his head. "Probably just a paranoid old man, but I have this bad feeling in my gut that we haven't seen the worst of Nicolas Kaplan yet."

"He's determined to get his hands on KJ," Bryson answered. "Nico doesn't give up when he sets his mind to something. After all he's been tracking and harassing Tasha for more than thirty years."

They all entered the cabin, and Rudy led them back to a large guest bedroom with a cozy-looking bed, and only one small window. The glass pane was missing, and in its place was a large sheet of plywood. There was a bathroom just outside the bedroom door, and even though the building was small, it housed everything necessary.

"You three can use my cabin until we leave, I've pretty much packed up everything I'm taking already, and I'm going to bunk down with the O'Brien brothers," Rudy said, as he went into another room and picked up a large duffel bag.

"Thank you, Rudy," Thomas said, laying KJ down on the bed, and brushing the hair off her face.

"Don't thank me until you've mated your girl there. Graham is right, Doc, if you want to protect her, then you have to be as strong as the enemy. I can't relate to what you're feeling, because I've been a wolf all my life, but know this, wolf or not, you're already part of our family because our Katie loves you."

With that Rudy turned and left the cabin, leaving a stunned Bryson and Thomas standing guard over the sleeping woman. Bryson noted the lines etched into Thomas's face that hadn't been there yesterday, and the dark rings of exhaustion and tension that were under his eyes. This was putting a lot of stress on him, and Bryson was feeling a bit edgy himself about being pushed into mating. It wasn't that he didn't want KJ, no, he wanted her with every fiber of his being, but mating was serious. He wasn't going to force her into something she couldn't take back. They would mate her when she was ready, and not before.

"He's right," Thomas said with a loud sigh.

Bryson glared at him. "What? You just said you wouldn't force her!"

"No, I mean he's right about Nicolas. There is no way the man is going to just walk away from this fight, and that means that there will be another battle." Thomas began pulling his clothes off, and then settled onto the bed with KJ.

Bryson still stood in the bedroom doorway, but he watched as KJ instinctively curled into Thomas's body, and snuggled her face into his shoulder. His wolf was howling in his head trying to make him go climb into bed with them, but he resisted.

"Hey, I think I'm going to find something to eat real quick. I'll come back in a few minutes," Bryson said, and Thomas frowned at him.

"Are you okay, Bry?"

He nodded. "Yeah, I just…I guess I just need a breather. I'll be back shortly." With that he spun around and walked back out into the living room of the cabin. This whole series of events had left him feeling chaotic and he needed to think. Had it really only been hours since he'd met KJ and Thomas? Just a day ago he was a Kaplan Omega wolf on a mission to collect Katie Jo Whetstone and return her to her parents' birth pack. Now he was fighting to keep her out of his Alpha's hands. It was ridiculous and terrifying all at once.

Bryson had dreamed of getting out of Alaska and seeing the world for so long, and now he was going to be tied down to Kansas City with a mate and a…whatever Thomas was to him. His mom would be ecstatic to hear that he had found his true mate, and his wolf was clearly all in, but was he?

He thought about the beautiful blonde-haired, blue-eyed wolf that fought with such intensity for what she wanted. She was protective and loyal to her pack, but last night he had seen that she was also self-conscious and vulnerable. The fact that she remained a virgin at twenty-four when she was so beautiful blew his mind and made him feel even more protective of her. She had saved that part of herself for her mate, and he and Thomas were just lucky enough to be on the receiving end of it.

His wolf butted against his chest and growled in his head.

Mate.

Yeah, I hear you. I want her too, but I need to give her space to decide.

Mate.

It's not that simple.

Mate.

There was no point in arguing with his other half over something that he couldn't control. If KJ made a move then he would gladly take it, but until she gave the go-ahead, he was going to hold his wolf back one way or another. Dreams be damned, he was falling in love.

Set on his decision, he headed for the kitchen and rooted through the cabinets until he found a box of cereal. Munching on the sugary cereal gave him something to do, as he wandered through the cabin checking out the layout and security. There were very few windows, and the master bedroom had another large sheet of plywood nailed over the one window in it. The bedroom door also had an oversized deadbolt on it. Rudy had been prepared for an invasion at some point. The reality of how dangerous the situation was finally struck a chord inside of Bryson, and his stomach tightened into a ball.

If Nico got his hands on KJ again, she was dead. He knew enough about the man to know that there was a good chance that Nico was planning another attack on the camp now that KJ had arrived, so the best option was to get them all out of here as quickly as possible. Trying to load up all these people into two vans, and transport them was going to be a challenge.

With a sigh of frustration, and a shake of his head, he walked back to the bedroom that contained his mate. Thomas had managed to divest KJ of her clothing while she slept, and he too was asleep now. They looked content curled up together, but Bryson's wolf pushed him forward until he was climbing into the bed on the other side. Scooting in, he pressed his chest up against KJ's back. Her scent filled his nose, and his cock grew rock hard. The memory of how her slick heat had enveloped him last night had him groaning low in his throat, and he tried to count sheep in his head to tame his libido until sleep took him.

KJ woke to the encompassing warmth of two large male bodies. Her cheek was pressed against Thomas's chest, the crisp black hairs tickling her nose, while Bryson's arm rested in the curve of her waist, and the length of his body warmed her backside. It was a perfect cocoon of love and protection, and her wolf was almost content. She was still pushing for the complete mating.

The old stories of wolves going out of their minds when denied their mates flitted through her brain, but she pushed the thoughts aside. Surely that was just an old wives' tale, and it wasn't like she was really denying them. It was very likely that they would mate soon. She just wasn't sure that she would be completely happy with never seeing the world. What if Thomas and Bryson turned into overprotective wolves just like all those, she had spent her whole life with, and never let her out of the den? She would be well loved and well cared for but coddled and hovered over just like she had been for twenty-four years. Her heart ached with the need to stretch past her limits and get away from the invisible fences that held her captive. With two mates, she just couldn't see how that would ever be possible.

Snippets of her mother telling her how happy she would be to find a mate and settle down to raise a family reminded her of the situation at hand. Her mother was dying. Thomas hadn't wanted to tell her that outright, but she could read between the lines. When Tasha died, Graham would follow with a broken heart. She was going to have to face it, and move forward without the only two people that she had ever been able to trust.

She surveyed the situation with what she hoped was an open mind. Thomas was like many of the wolves she had met at the Gray Pack den. He was dominating, and protective to the extreme, but he was also genuinely sweet and loving. Bryson was his opposite. The light to Thomas's dark. He was a jokester, playing and laughing, but his protective nature was just as strong. Bryson seemed to have some self-esteem issues based on his place in life, while Thomas felt inadequate when surrounded by werewolves who were stronger and faster than he was. Both were delicious in looks, and their imperfections were perfect in their own ways. She couldn't deny anymore that she had very strong feelings for both of them and would be lost without them. Now, facing losing both of her parents, at least she would have the two of them to hold her when she cried.

"You're thinking too hard, little one," Thomas whispered, and she tipped her head to look up at him. In the dim light of the room she was unable to distinguish his expression, but his body was relaxed and comforting under her cheek. The shadows made him look dark and dangerous as the late afternoon sunlight filtered through the crack at the top of the plywood-covered window frame.

"What do you dream of, Thomas?" she asked.

She could feel him grinning, and his body shook a little with a chuckle. "You mean what *was* I dreaming of while I slept? Well I have a naked goddess plastered against me, and a hard-on from hell, so—"

Slapping his chest, she huffed. "No, I mean what do you *dream* of? What do you want for your life?"

He was quiet for a few moments as he thought about it. "I've always dreamed of helping people. That was part of the reason I became a doctor in the first place. When I was a kid, I used to pretend to be a doctor in a faraway country where no one knew that I was just a regular old guy from Missouri, instead, in my dreams, I was their hero. Saving their lives, and healing their sick…that probably sounds ridiculous, but I was a kid."

"Dreams are never ridiculous," Bryson rumbled, and KJ jumped a little. "Sorry, peaches, I thought you knew I was awake. It's not like I could sleep when there's a philosophical discussion happening in my bed."

She elbowed him and turned her attention back to Thomas. "You wanted to travel?"

"Yeah, I suppose so. I don't know. I have always figured I would have a wife and kids by now, so traveling wouldn't work out, but for the last couple years I've kind of been circling the drain waiting for something big to happen. I had no idea it would come in the form of a hot little she-wolf."

She giggled, and Bryson laughed loudly. "Yeah, we really lucked out in that sense. I never thought I'd end up with a fifties pinup for my mate."

"A pinup?" she questioned, as she snickered at him. "Yeah right. Only for a dartboard."

Without warning she was suddenly on her back, with two irritated men looming over her. Even with just a hint of sunlight in the room, she caught the flashing of Bryson's green eyes.

"No talking badly about yourself, little one. We warned you about that," Thomas said sounding rather menacing.

"Thanks, peaches. I've been dying to spank that beautiful ass of yours, and you just gave us the reason we needed," Bryson said with glee.

She growled in her throat. "You are *not* spanking me." Even as she said it, she felt the flutter of desire in her belly. She wanted them to take her and do whatever they wanted to her. The idea of a spanking was a little intimidating, but it was surprisingly attractive too. Just feeling their hands on her body was a good thing to her wolf, who preened in her head.

Thomas's hands were fast, and before she could argue further, she was flipped onto her stomach with Bryson straddling her thighs, and Thomas holding her wrists together above her head.

"What the hell? You can't double-team me!" she yelled, thrashing as she tried to unseat Bryson.

"That's the thing, peaches. The best part about a ménage is that there will be twice the manpower to bring you back under control when you get out of hand." His palm came down on her ass with a resounding crack, and she yelped. It burned like crazy, but it sent a sizzle of electricity to her pussy, making her clench her ass cheeks together. "Oh baby, clench again. That's fucking hot. How can you say you're not beautiful? Look at this peach colored skin, Tom, isn't it perfect?"

"Every inch, Bry," Thomas said softly. She craned her neck to look up at him and felt her own core melt at the heat in his gaze. How could she not fall in love with these two men? They could take her from laughing to burning up in a second, and they looked so damn good doing it.

Previously, Thomas's facial hair was neatly groomed but after the last twenty-four hours of chaos it now looked slightly unkempt, and she ached to feel it on her skin. Bryson's large hands were circling and squeezing her ass cheeks, making her arch up into him with the hope that he would ease the throbbing in her clit.

"Are you just going to look at it, Rambo? Or you do you plan on doing something with it?" she said over her shoulder.

Bryson stopped moving and started to laugh low in his throat. "Oh, peaches, that's a hell of a dare. Have I mentioned yet how much I love dares?" His breath was hot against her ear, and she shivered. Suddenly he was gripping her hips tightly and lifting her up. "On your knees, baby. You want me to do something with that ass, then I will definitely be fulfilling your request."

His hand came down on her prone cheeks with a sharp slap, and she cursed.

"No cursing," Thomas said as he shifted his weight underneath the front of her body. Her wrists were still gripped in his, but now her face hovered over the top of his crotch. His hard cock pointed straight up at her, and she didn't hesitate for long. Darting her tongue out, she teased the tip of him, while Bryson slapped her butt again, and then slid a finger down into her folds.

"Fuck, she's flooding the place, Tom! We're going to have to put all that cream to good use." KJ started to ask what he was talking about, when his finger teased her asshole gently. She gasped, and Thomas slid his cockhead into her open mouth, and then met her eyes with a challenging grin. Swallowing hard around him, she began to bob her head, as she tensed against Bryson's playing fingers.

Bryson had never played with a virgin's asshole. KJ was pretty and pink from front to back, and her little rosette was closed up tight. He felt his balls tighten in response as he dipped the tip of his finger into her passage and she squealed a little bit around Thomas's cock. Easing back so he didn't frighten her, he pressed kisses on her rounded ass and nipped gently at the skin until his canine teeth dropped and he was afraid he would mate her by accident.

He sunk his finger into her sopping wet pussy and then pressed it into her ass, going deeper this time. She moaned instead of squealing, and he grinned at Thomas over her head. It was a good sign that she liked it, had she not it might have made this whole ménage relationship trickier. Setting up a rhythm of thrusting his finger in and out of her tight hole, he rose up on his knees and pressed his throbbing cock against her pussy. The slick folds opened for him like a flower, and he was buried balls deep before he could even think clearly.

Using his own knees, he spread her thighs wider, causing her to arch her back and cock her hips up to him. The view was spectacular, as her curvy ass rose in the air to meet him, and his finger slid into the crack. Banging into her a little harder, he was pleased to feel her ass clench on his finger, and her greedy cunt sucking at his cock.

Thomas had released her wrists and was holding her head, pumping his cock into her mouth, while Bryson fucked into her pretty pussy. This was heaven. Being inside of her was absolutely perfect. By the sounds coming from her throat, she thought so, too. He paused long enough to sink a second finger into her tight bud, and then spread them, stretching the closed-up hole wider.

He wanted to fuck her ass, but he needed to work her into it. Hurting her wasn't even in his realm of possibility, and he also wanted to keep her enjoying this. Thomas suddenly groaned and thrust up into her mouth. KJ was bobbing like mad on his dick and clenching her body around Bryson until he was cross-eyed. Desperately trying to retain his control so he didn't come like a schoolboy, he eased his fingers out of her ass, and pulled her backward, away from Thomas's softening cock.

She ended up sitting in his lap, with her legs on either side of his hips, and her back to his chest. He cupped her breasts in both hands, squeezing hard, as she gasped, and bounced on his cock. Bryson let his eyes drift closed as he enjoyed her movements. She was helping herself, using him for her pleasure, and he couldn't be happier about it.

A shuffle of movement, and Bryson felt the brush of Thomas's finger against KJ's pussy. Tom was playing with KJ's clit while she rode Bryson's cock. Her pussy seemed to snap tighter, like a rubber band around him, and his wolf started to come to the forefront. He was going to lose control if she gave him the slightest opening.

All of a sudden, she did just that. Her head rocked to the side, exposing her long slim throat, and he did what nature expected him to do, sinking his fangs into her. She screamed with pleasure as he lapped at the blood that was leaking from her pale skin and poured his cum deep into her womb. The fact that such an intimate piece of him was inside of her, stretched his orgasm out until he wondered if his balls would bruise the next day.

She fell back against him limply, panting for breath after the powerful orgasm they shared. Bryson's heart was racing. She was his now. He had claimed her. Obviously, she still had to claim him back to complete the bond, but how was she going to feel, considering that he didn't ask her first? Thomas was staring at the bite wound in astonishment, and his eyes kept darting to KJ's face.

"Peaches, I'm not going to apologize," Bryson said against her skin, after placing a soft kiss on the already healing wound.

She crooked her neck to meet his gaze, and his breath caught at the emotions rolling through her blue eyes. "Why would you? We knew it would happen eventually, although I figured I would be claiming you at the same time. I guess we'll just have to play it by ear and let it happen when it happens."

Bryson gave her a smile as he lifted her off his lap and settled her on the bed next to Thomas. "When you're ready to claim me, you will, but there is no need to rush, love. I'm going to go take a quick shower, while Tom keeps you company."

She gave him a comforting smile and he pressed a sweet kiss on her soft lips. Sated and slightly loopy, she was so much freer with her heart, and he loved knowing that he had opened that door for her. When he stood to leave, she turned into Thomas's arms and they too shared a deep kiss that seemed to solidify the bond that the three of them were already forming.

He took one last long look at the lovers on the bed, before he turned and left the bedroom. This had to be heaven.

CHAPTER ELEVEN

The sound of a woman screaming and wolves snarling woke Thomas from a dead sleep. He could feel the ache in his muscles that came from hours of fucking, but his brain went on high alert instantly.

"Oh my God, that sounded like Kayla!" KJ gasped, and she shoved at Bryson's shoulder for him to move faster. Thomas rolled off the bed on his side, and slid his legs into his jeans, which were uncharacteristically still crumpled up on the bedroom floor. His heart was racing, and his throat felt slightly swollen. Whoever had screamed, it was a scream of fear, not pain. He had to be optimistic and just hope that there was some sort of unusually loud disagreement happening outside, instead of an attack by the Kaplans. Another scream outside shut down his fervent prayers, and it hit him that his worst fears were coming true. Nicolas Kaplan had sent his wolves into the den, and by the sounds of the fight, they were on a death mission.

KJ and Bryson were already out the door and down the hall, still naked. *I guess it wouldn't make much sense for them to get dressed when they are just going to shift.* Without warning, KJ stopped in her tracks and spun around to face him. Fear had turned her skin a pale gray color, and her normally blue eyes were dark like sapphires, the pupils nearly over-whelming them. "Doc, please stay here. I can't risk losing you."

"What? Are you kidding me? I'm not going to stay here while my woman goes running off into battle to protect me!" Thomas's blood was boiling. How could she look at him like that? It was like she pitied him for being just a weak human. Well this human was tougher than he looked, and he planned on proving it to whoever was out there making women scream.

"Tom, you can't fight off a wolf, man. Right now, it sounds like there are dozens of them out there. I know for a fact Kaplan brought more than thirty with him. Running into that while you're still human would be suicide. Do what KJ said and lock yourself in that back bedroom. Rudy had it set up for a freaking military invasion, so you should be safe." Bryson spoke while he moved, but when he reached the front door, he went into stealth mode, peeking through the window cautiously. "This is bad, guys. I count eleven from this view, but no doubt there are more around the bend."

"We brought seven wolves with us. KJ said there were twenty-two here already. That's pretty good odds, right?" Thomas was trying to temper his anger until they were out the door.

"It might have been an even match of forces if all our wolves were able to fight, but we have kids and injured wolves here. It won't be a blood bath, but it won't be easy." Thomas watched as Bryson surveyed the battle, they could hear raging outside. He could see Bryson's wolf fighting for control of his body. It was unreal. There was hair starting to sprout over his arms, thicker and coarser than his natural body hair, and his facial structure was shifting slightly. When Bryson turned his green eyes back to him, they had an eerie glow that only seemed to come when a werewolf was close to shifting.

"Oh shit! They have Ryley three to one! I have to get out there!" KJ had moved up under Bryson's arm to see for herself what was happening outside, and now he could see her body flickering in front of him. Half shifting, and then shifting back a millisecond later. He could feel the agitation and anger rolling off her, but when she looked back at him there was only concern for his well-being in their depths.

"Bryson go! KJ can stay here with me." The idea of letting her run out into a mass of angry warring wolves made his blood run cold. If anyone needed to be protected it was her.

"What? No way! I'm a wolf, damn it. And I've been fighting the Kaplans all my life. I'm going out there, but I'm not sure I can think straight in a fight if I'm worried about you, Doc." His heart broke for her, as he realized that outside the door, her family was being attacked, and how he would react if it was Tina, or his parents out there.

"Go. I'll be fine. Shift, and go do what you need to. I'll be right behind you, and I promise you, that I will be fine." Inhaling to push his chest out, he tried to make his body look even bigger and meaner. He needed them to respect him as a human and understand that they couldn't coddle him. It wasn't like he was a child, he was a grown man, who had been training in martial arts and boxing for years. He could throw down when necessary and based on the sharp yelp and snapping of teeth he could hear, it was definitely going to be necessary.

KJ stared into his eyes for another long second, battling with her need to protect him, and protect her family simultaneously, before she nodded and shifted. A breath later, her wolf eyes were staring up into his human ones, and she nodded one more time before she turned back to Bryson.

Bryson looked agitated and he huffed. "Fine, whatever, just don't get yourself killed. I have a feeling that ice would be pretty damn pissed at me if you end up d—"

His last words cut off as he shifted into his animal skin, and the two wolves burst from the cabin into the melee that was happening outside without another backward glance. Thomas stood in the doorway trying to grasp the situation and get his bearings. The problem he had now was that they were all in wolf form, so he couldn't always tell who was who. Some of them he knew. Cash was to his right in his wolf form, and nearby, Owen's chestnut brown fur caught his eye. The two brothers fought almost back to back against three other wolves that were smaller, and seemingly quicker. They worked efficiently, dispatching the three wolves without much trouble. Just as it seemed the battle was won, two more wolves were on them, appearing from out of nowhere through the trees. It was almost as if they waited in waves to attack, but that was an illogical battle plan, right?

As he watched a mottled brown wolf take a swipe at Rafe who was attempting to help his cousins, Thomas realized that it was in fact a brilliant plan. If Nicolas sent his wolves in a few at a time, he would eventually exhaust the strongest wolves—the Gray Pack wolves. Once they grew tired, they would be vulnerable, and it would allow the Kaplan Pack to gain the upper hand.

Turning from them he noted where Noah, Luke, and Ryley were, but now he had lost sight of KJ and Bryson. Fear settled deep in his belly. A brief thought flitted through his brain that Bryson might have been playing them all and helped with capturing KJ. As quickly as it hit him, he dismissed it. Bryson may not be perfect, but he wasn't a traitor, and Thomas believed in his heart that Bryson was in love with KJ. There was no way he would do anything to intentionally risk her, and giving her to Nicolas Kaplan was beyond the realm of possibility.

However, that didn't mean that the other Kaplan wolves couldn't get their hands on her, while Bryson was distracted. Nicolas had made it clear that he needed her alive, so collecting her would be the Kaplan wolves' highest priority. Suddenly feeling like he and Bryson had made a grave error in allowing her out into the open, he shot out the door in the direction his mate and partner had gone.

Growls and snarls rumbled around him, sending shivers of anxiety down his spine. One bite of those powerful jaws could maim him or kill him. He was careful to avoid stepping into any of the small battles happening around him, until he saw two wolves had a very small gray wolf pinned against the side of a cabin. The little wolf was either female or a child still, but it was unfamiliar to him. He watched in horror as the wolf was unable to avoid their snapping jaws and yelped when one of them clamped down on her flank.

Thomas reacted without another thought and sunk his hands into the fur of the attacking wolf. Gripping it tightly, he swung the wolf with all his strength, ripping it off the smaller wolf, and tossing it behind him. The second attacker came at him with snapping teeth, and death in his gold eyes. Thomas refused to back down, and he threw his best uppercut into the wolf's jaw, stopping it in its tracks. Without a whimper the wolf collapsed into a limp pile of fur in front of him, and Thomas nearly howled with delight. He had fought a wolf and won. It was a victory he would savor, and possibly rub in his woman's face later.

A snarl was the only warning, before the first wolf attacked him from the back. His teeth scraped down Thomas's spine leaving a burning trail of pain. Arching as far away from the animal as possible, he threw himself to the ground trying to escape from the vicious canines that were snapping at him. Rolling away from the injured wolf that he had been trying to protect, he couldn't stop the groan of pain when the attacking wolf bit down into his vulnerable side. He felt his ribs crack, and the intensity of the burn in his belly assured him that he was bleeding internally. Being a doctor really sucked sometimes, because it meant that in this moment, he knew he was dying before anyone else did. Twisting himself, he threw his arm out with every bit of strength he had left, reaching for the wolf's vulnerable throat. When the animal let out a surprised yelp, Thomas knew that he had hit his mark. A choking, rasping sound was now coming from the injured animal, and he watched as its eyes widened in fear and understanding. The broken windpipe was a slow painful death, but again, he had managed to stop a vicious animal.

"See you in hell, asshole," he whispered, as the light went out of the wolf's eyes. Adrenaline was pumping through his veins, keeping the pain at bay, but the moment all was quiet, he groaned loudly in frustration. "Fucking hell!" he screamed at the sky, wanting everyone and no one to hear him. "Just when I finally find a piece of happiness, I managed to get myself killed."

"Thomas!"

The voice was hollow, like it was from a distance, but he turned his head toward it automatically. A flash of gold and then KJ's scent filled his nose bringing him some peace.

"KJ?" He managed to lift his hand to cup her soft cheek, but he could feel it trembling. His other hand was still pressed to the wound in his side as he tried to hold his own life in for a little bit longer. It just figured that he finally found love, and she had to watch him die now.

KJ stared down at Thomas in horror. He was covered in blood and surrounded by dead Kaplan wolves. Tugging his large hand away from his bleeding side, she felt the tears well up in her eyes when she saw the blood streaming from his body. It was bad, fatal if Thomas was correct in his assessment.

Her stomach heaved, as she stared at the deep wound in his abdomen. She could only see the top teeth marks, which meant that the bottom teeth marks were in his back. Someone dangled a shirt in front of her, and she took it, pressing it to the wound firmly, and trying not to pass out.

"No! Oh my God, no! You can't die on me, Doc. I just decided to keep you, so you don't get the option of dying! I need you!" She raged at him with tears on her cheeks. Her pain was soul deep, and her lungs felt like they were closing up on her. Her wolf howled in her ears, screaming in pain for its dying mate.

"Tom! Holy shit! What have you done to yourself? Peaches, move over, and let me look at him. We need to get him into the cabin so we can get him fixed up." Bryson tried to physically move her, but Thomas shook his head, stopping him. KJ looked up into Bryson's worried face feeling like someone had just carved her heart out of her body and dropped it on the ground. Cash and the other Gray wolves stood with most of the Quiver Creek Pack watching with sadness and regret etched onto their faces.

"No, Bry. Taking me in and stitching me up isn't going to be enough, and I—" Thomas choked on his words and coughed as blood spilled out of the corner of his mouth.

"Tom, let us try. Damn it, man. We told you to stay in the fucking house! Why the hell did you even try to fight those wolves?" Bryson asked, pressing down on Thomas's side, trying everything he could to stop the flow of blood, as KJ gripped his hand against her breasts and cried silent tears.

"He was saving me!" Rose Griffin stepped forward, and KJ could see she had a bite wound over her hip. "It was two on one, and Doc stepped in. If it weren't for his quick thinking I would have died. He's a hero."

"What the hell were you doing out here, Rosey Posey? You should have been in the storm shelter with the other kids!" Samson held his daughter against his chest, rocking her as she shook with her adrenaline.

"I had to help! Dad, they killed Kelly and Brick! I saw them, Brick was being torn to pieces, and Kelly tried to help him. It was so scary, Dad!" Rose's voice broke into sobs, and a sound of anguish rose from the group.

"Oh my God! Sam, that's three of us! Zara was the one on rounds when they first attacked. They took her out just as soon as she sounded the warning." Kayla's voice was quiet and tight.

"Rudy is gone, too. I couldn't get to him, they took out his throat." River O'Brien's face was a ghastly shade of gray, and KJ tried to compute what he was saying. They were talking about her family members. People who were dead. Her family members were dead. Rudy. Zara. Brick. Kelly. Was it possible?

KJ could hear the others muttering around her, but she couldn't make out their words anymore. All she knew was that the love she had just begun to accept and let into her heart was seeping out of her as quickly as Thomas's blood was staining the dirt around him. "No! You won't be a martyr. Fuck that! We're going to do the claiming right now, and then you will shift. You can heal as a wolf."

Without waiting for permission, or encouragement, she bent and latched onto Thomas's shoulder with her canine teeth. Sinking her sharp teeth into his skin, she tasted his tangy blood on her tongue, just as warmth filled her body, sending the burn of desire straight to her clit. His groan of satisfaction was tempered with the pain his body was fighting. She lifted her head and held his chin in her hand.

"Thomas Jameson look at me. I love you, and you are mine. I won't give you up. Please, bite me, I need you. Please!" She waited for another second as emotions and pain rolled through his dark chocolate eyes. When he nodded his agreement, she turned and tilted her head, pressing her neck against his mouth. His strength was fading fast based on the first tentative nip he placed there, but then a sharp sting hit her as he bit through her skin.

It wasn't the ideal setting for a claiming, but she knew that with the bond came the shift to a wolf, as well as the strength and healing qualities they possessed. As her blood spilled into his mouth, her wolf was howling with a combination of pleasure and agony. The sweetest heat filled her belly and stole her breath, making her moan softly. He pulled away and stared back at her in awe. Love lit the brown pools, and he gave her a small grin.

"Thank you, little one. I love you too. Bryson take care of her for me," Thomas said, coughing again. More blood dribbled from his mouth and KJ wailed.

"No! I claimed you! You have to shift now!"

She felt hands on her waist, and she flailed as Bryson wrapped himself around her body and tugged her away from Thomas. Screaming at her mate to let her go back to his side, she watched as Ryley, Cash, and Samson helped gently lift Thomas from the ground and carried him into the cabin they stood next to. She pounded on Bryson, and threw her legs back trying to get free from his viselike grip. Her wolf and her human both wanted nothing more than to hold her mate in her arms and help him through the change. If he could shift, he would live. She just needed him to shift.

Bryson felt like the worst kind of man in the world as his mate cursed his soul to hell and fought with every fiber of her being to get to Thomas's side. His eyes lifted to Rafe's, who nodded, and Bryson held her tightly.

Still holding KJ against his chest as she sobbed and shook with emotion, Bryson followed everyone into the cabin. Every few moments she would lash out, trying to escape his grasp and get to Thomas. It didn't look good for him. The amount of blood he was losing alone was terrifying.

Once Thomas was settled on top of the large dining table, Graham stepped to his side, and pulled the clothing off his body trying to see the wound. Bryson allowed KJ to move to Thomas's side and help her father tend to him, thinking that if Thomas was going to die, then he deserved to have his last moments with his mate.

Cash stepped up to Bryson and put his hand on his shoulder. "I need to talk to you."

"Right now? I don't want to leave her——" Bryson started to protest, but something on the cowboy's face had him following him to the front porch.

Ryley and Rafe stepped out behind them, with Noah, Luke, and Owen on their heels. "This better be good, Cash." Ryley growled. "My sister is in there watching her mate die, and we should be with her."

"I have a plan, but you aren't going to like it," Cash said, and Bryson felt his stomach drop to his feet. "We need to force him to shift. There are only two ways to force a wolf to shift, threaten him…"

"Or threaten his mate," Bryson finished quietly, his voice vibrating with rage. "No! You're not going to put her in danger! I won't let you!"

Rafe stepped in between Bryson and Cash, forcing them apart. "Before you tear him to pieces, remember the pain that she is feeling, Bryson."

Bryson's mouth fell open, and his eyes widened, "Have you all lost your minds? What do you plan to do? Hold a gun to her head?"

Cash shook his head. "No, we have to get her scared enough that she will scream for help and his wolf will respond. We have to give her to Kaplan."

Bryson saw red and lunged at Cash. His wolf came forward, shifting to the surface as he lashed out at his new pack mate. The threat to KJ was enough to make him lose his mind. This was the most insane plan he had ever heard, and the fact that Cash thought he would just go with it was ludicrous.

Hands landed on his neck, and a pair of arms wrapped around his middle. Before he knew it he was completely and irrevocably restrained by members of the Gray Pack. They were going to do it with or without him. They were going to betray KJ.

"No! You're going to get her killed! I'll rip your throat out, motherfucker!"

Cash knew as soon as KJ sunk her teeth into Thomas that this was the moment Delaky had been trying to prepare him for. He had to betray KJ and his new pack mates in order to protect a piece of his family. He couldn't just sit back, and watch Thomas die. This was the only solution. Owen, Luke, and Noah helped Rafe and Ryley restrain Bryson who was half-shifted into wolf form. The pain in Bryson's eyes was enough to make Cash's blood run cold.

The gravity of his plan sunk in as he turned and entered the cabin. Without meeting anyone's eyes, he walked over to KJ, who had climbed onto the table, and tucked herself against Thomas's uninjured side. She was begging and pleading with her mate, trying to find a way to get him to shift on demand. If only it was that easy.

Taking a final deep breath, he met Thomas's eyes as he bent slightly, and reassured by the approval he saw there, he scooped KJ up in his arms and ran. He pushed himself, trying hard to ignore the feral hellcat in his arms. He loved this little girl like she was his own sister, so hearing her curse him to hell and farther was painful. There was no other choice, so he kept moving. Past Bryson who screamed at him to stop, and into the woods.

KJ was screaming and pleading with him to stop. "What the hell are you doing, Cash? Let me go! Thomas needs me! Let me go you stupid asshole! Where are you taking me?"

She continued to berate him as he carried her further into the woods and away from the cabin that held the doc. KJ's screams got louder, and more desperate, but Cash refused to let her go. Pain laced his own heart and he felt like every step was hell on earth as he moved away. Bryson's words echoed in his ears.

You're going to get her killed!

Although he knew that this was the fastest way to force the doc to shift into his new form, he couldn't have known how hard it would be to carry her in the direction he knew the Kaplan wolves were. He could smell them, and his own wolf fought against his actions.

His wolf was snarling in anger at him as he deliberately moved toward danger with his captive, risking her in order to save Doc. If it worked it was genius, but if it didn't work…Well, he couldn't think about that right now.

A howl to his right stopped his forward motion, and KJ went still in his arms. Her face was tear streaked, and swollen, and Thomas's blood was still on her lips as she went pale.

"Cash?"

"I'm sorry KJ, but I have to—"

A Kaplan wolf darted from the trees into their path and snarled at Cash as it shifted. "Well, well, well. What do we have here?"

"Move, wolf. I need to see Nicolas Kaplan, and I don't have time for your shit."

Cash's heart was pounding as he realized that there were more Kaplan wolves just a couple hundred yards away. If this wolf sounded the alarm there would be no going back. Even if Thomas shifted, he wouldn't be able to rescue them both from the middle of the Kaplans again. It was just dumb luck that Bryson had managed to free them the first time.

"Cash?" KJ's voice was weak and confused as she looked from the tall rangy wolf in front of them and back to Cash. "What is going on?"

"I'm taking you to the Kaplans," he said flatly, and her face paled.

The strange wolf roared with laughter. "What? You aren't man enough to handle a hot she-wolf so you're giving her to real men?"

"Shut up you dumb fuck! Go back to your patrol and let us pass." KJ was stiff in his arms, but she wasn't fighting him anymore. If she shut down and refused to scream, then Thomas wouldn't know she was in danger and wouldn't shift. *Fuck, this was a terrible plan!*

"You're giving me to him? To Nicolas? But, why?" she said in a whisper, looking fragile and vulnerable.

It was on the tip of his tongue to deny it, and tell her what he was actually doing, but if he diverted from the plan now, Thomas was as good as dead. "Yes. In fact,"—he swallowed hard before he ground the words out— "this wolf can just take you with him. If I go carry you into that camp, I'm probably dead. This solves that problem."

Cash could have sworn that KJ stopped breathing for a moment as her eyes went wide, and then narrowed. He refused to meet her gaze, turning instead to the gleeful-looking stranger. "Here, you take her."

Just as Cash went to transfer KJ to the wolf's waiting arms, she fulfilled her part of the plan, and let out an ear curdling howl for help. Cash had to bite the inside of his cheek to keep from grinning. The Kaplan wolf, however, was flustered by her reaction, and didn't get a good grip on her. The moment Cash's arms left her body she twisted out of his hands and dropped to the ground on all fours.

She snarled as the other wolf grabbed for her hair, stopping her mid-shift, and wrapped his hand in it tightly, making her whimper in pain. "Hell no, sweet cheeks! You're not depriving me of the reward Nico is going to give to whoever brings you in!"

She yelped in pain right before a large black wolf barreled into the Kaplan wolf's side, knocking them both to the ground. Cash's sigh of relief was audible as he watched Thomas rip the throat out of the wolf that was hurting his mate. KJ sat in all her naked glory, staring at the two wolves in shock. When Thomas finally let go of the dead animal's body, and let his body fall limply to the ground, she gasped and laughed.

"Thomas! You did it! You shifted!" She threw her arms around the bloody wolf, who turned angry eyes on Cash.

"Whoa, man! I had to do it! If I didn't put her in danger, you wouldn't have shifted in time." Cash backed up quickly to keep his distance for the moment, as both KJ and Thomas glared daggers at him.

The accusation on KJ's face was heartbreaking, but Cash knew he had done the right thing. He couldn't just let a member of his family die without trying everything. And it had worked, so they should be grateful, not pissed off.

A howl sounded nearby, triggering Cash's self-preservation mode. "Sorry ladies and gents, but the war is about to be kicked into high gear. We're way too close to their pack for comfort considering you just killed one of them. Get your asses up and let's move!"

Cash shifted into his wolf and waited just long enough to make sure that both wolves were well ahead of him before he followed them to the relative safety of the Quiver Creek den and their family.

CHAPTER TWELVE

$\mathcal{K}$elly and Brick Poplin had two young sons. They were fantastic parents, and loyal to the Quiver Creek Pack of misfits. Zara Todd was a mom as well, to Justus and Fabian. Justus was sixteen and Fabian was only eight. All four children now faced the grief that came with losing their parents.

KJ could hardly stand to face them as the remaining pack members came together in the Whetstone cabin once more. The four wolves that were lost in the battle, along with the dozen Kaplan wolves that were found dead throughout the den, were buried just east of the cabin line. It actually made her physically sick to know that the Kaplans didn't even reclaim their dead. They just left them to rot in the sun. It was horrifying and reminded her just how lucky she was that she hadn't actually been captured by them again.

The loss of so many of their pack mates had taken its toll on everyone. Her mother and father especially seemed to be at a loss as to how to face life without Rudy in it. He had been a sort of leader and figurehead for their little pack, an unofficial Alpha of sorts. There was no doubt in KJ's mind that Rudy died exactly how he would have chosen, but it didn't take the sting away.

Thomas had been in his wolf form for hours. His body had to have time to heal, and until it was well rested, he couldn't shift back. After warning Cash that they would hash it out later, Bryson had stuck by her side like glue, supporting her in every way as she went about the business of consoling her family and grieving. At the moment she was seated in Bryson's lap, with his arms banded tightly around her middle, and Thomas's head resting on her thigh. She stroked her fingers through his midnight-colored fur, marveling at the beauty of his wolf form. He matched the other Gray Pack wolves in size, but they were stunned to realize that his eyes changed color when he shifted. Instead of their normal melted chocolate color, they lightened into a brilliant amber that had swirls of chocolate brown throughout.

Glancing up, she watched as her dad settled her mother into a comfortable chair, before standing behind her like a guard dog. Her mom had weakened significantly, and it looked like she wasn't going to be able to travel with them to Kansas City. How KJ was going to face leaving her mother was anyone's guess.

"I'm not exactly sure that I have the right words for this." Graham paused, swallowing hard. "Losing Rudy, Zara, Brick, and Kelly…Well, it feels like they've cut one of our arms off and we're trying to figure out how to get it reattached. The truth is that it's never going to happen. We have to learn how to support ourselves with the other arm and move forward."

Wesley Todd let out a loud, empty laugh that echoed with grief for his dead wife, and KJ felt hot tears on her own cheeks. What do you say to a man who'd just lost his wife, and had to raise his two sons on his own? KJ felt guilt that she felt relief in knowing that Wesley and Zara were not bond mates. It meant that at least Fabian and Justus would have one of their parents to lean on. Had they been true mates instead of just in love, it would have been Wesley's death sentence too.

"Graham, I understand the need for sensitivity, but we have to get everyone moved back to Kansas City as quickly as possible. We don't know for sure how long we have before the Kaplans come after us again." Samson met Graham's eyes steadily. Always the reasonable one, Samson had been scared out of his mind at how close he had been to losing one of his children. KJ had never seen the giant man so emotionally frazzled.

"We have to wait until Tasha can—"

Tasha cut her husband off. "No, Graham, they can't wait. What is the purpose of waiting around for a dead woman? I intend to stay here at Quiver Creek until I finally breathe my last breath. However, I want to see my children safely off before I do so. Rafe, Ryley, Katie Jo, I can only imagine how difficult this is for you, but I need you to accept that I know my own body. I am dying. I can't make it to Kansas City, so instead I will enjoy my final moments with my husband."

"Mama, Thomas said that he could do the surgery…" KJ stopped when her mother turned her sad eyes her way and shook her head.

"Katie Jo, you will go back with all them, taking your brave mates with you, and building a life that you can be proud of. The Gray Pack will protect you from Nicolas Kaplan, and you will not have to fight for every step forward like I have. Please, move on. For me."

It was impossible to deny her mother anything, but more so when she looked so lost and sad. KJ could only nod her agreement. Rafe, however, had a different approach. Standing and moving across the room, he dropped to his knees in front of Tasha, taking her hands into his, and staring into her eyes.

"Tasha…Mom…maybe this is wrong, it's probably extremely self-ish, but damn it you owe Ryley and I time with you. I can't deny that I'm angry, and I'm still trying to forgive you. I don't know how to have more than one set of parents, but I'm not willing to let you give up without trying everything. At least do us the favor of traveling back to the den and attempting the surgery. I want my wife Shandi to meet you."

There wasn't a dry eye in the room, as Rafe knelt in front of the mother who hadn't been there physically for him growing up. KJ could understand her older brother's anger and frustration at Tasha. Honestly, she didn't know if she would have been strong enough to forgive their parents if the situation were reversed.

Tasha and Rafe shared a silent moment that seemed almost too personal to watch. After several breaths, Tasha's weakened body slumped into the chair and she nodded her agreement. It was almost as though Rafe had taken the burden of deciding her fate onto his own wide shoulders, so she didn't have to carry it anymore. The big man held his arms out and for only the second time in more than twenty years he gave his birth mother a hug. KJ's heart lifted at the pure joy that broke over Tasha's face. There had to be salvation at the end of this miserable path, right? Fate couldn't be so unforgiving as to steal Tasha and Graham away after it just took four other family members from them.

"So it's settled. We leave tomorrow morning for Kansas City." Ryley's voice cracked with emotion as he watched his older brother holding his mother tightly. "Everyone needs to go back to their cabins or beds and double-check that they have all their personal belongings. Nothing more than you must have to survive, because we don't have a lot of room."

"Gamma Tasha?" KJ's heart stopped in her throat, when little Axel Poplin spoke from where he was settled in Lily Griffin's arms.

"Yes, darling?" Tasha pulled away to face Axel, and opened her arms to him. He climbed out of Lily's lap and made his way into Tasha's.

"Gamma, where am I gonna go? Am I gonna go to heaven like Mommy and Daddy?" Axel's pale green eyes were filled with worry and fear, and his words caused more tension in the room.

Tasha seemed too choked up to speak, as she held the child against her breast. "Oh no, darling. You aren't going to go to heaven for many many years to come. You're going to stay with your pack, well, with your new pack. There will be a place for you."

Rafe who still knelt in front of Tasha and Axel reached out and tipped the boy's face, so he met his eyes. "Axel, how old are you, son?"

Axel sniffed and wiped his nose on his sleeve. "I'm four and three quarters. My little brother Jordy is only three, but I take care of him."

Chuckles rumbled through the room at the fierce sibling loyalty in the statement. His childish voice made the word sound more like free instead of three, but the message came through.

"Hmm…four and three quarters, huh? Well, see, my brother and I just married this beautiful princess back home, and we are looking for a couple boys to be our sons. I was thinking we needed someone about five years old though, because we need someone who is made of tough stuff." Rafe paused as though he was thinking hard about the decision, but his challenge had perked Axel right up.

"I'm tough! I'm tougher than any five-year-old I know! Could I be your son?" His eyes widened with hope and he puffed his little chest out like a champion.

"I think that might work out all right. Do you think you would like to have two dads?" Rafe asked, and Axel frowned. His tiny tongue peeked out between his lips as he thought about the options.

"Can Jordy come too?"

Ryley stepped over and bent to be eye level with Axel. "We definitely want Jordan, too."

Axel turned back to Tasha. "Gamma, did ya hear that? I'm gonna have two daddies, and Jordy is coming too! And we get to have a princess for a mama!"

"I heard, darling! I heard!" Tears spilled down Tasha's face, and KJ sobbed loudly in Bryson's arms.

To watch Axel gain so much pleasure out of such a small thing just warmed her soul. Losing so many lives seemed so worthless until the silver lining peeked through the clouds. KJ knew that Shandi wasn't able to have kids because of her cancer treatments. That had been a point of contention between her and the guys when they first met. To hear that they would be willing to take in the two boys that were like nephews to her already melted the rest of the barrier she had erected between her heart and accepting her brothers. They were all going to go to Kansas City to the Gray Pack den and build a new life. One way or another.

With everything settled, the wolves all scattered to go finish their packing, or tuck the little ones into bed. Axel didn't want to leave

Rafe's side until he promised to come and give him a goodnight hug after a few minutes.

The moment the room was cleared of all but Tasha, Graham, KJ, Bryson, and the original Gray Pack members, Bryson nudged KJ off his lap. He looked down at Thomas and gave a sharp nod. To KJ's surprise, Thomas shifted immediately, and stood to his full height. There was a light pink ridge around the side of him, from just below his ribs to his hip bone, but it was healing well. He bent and dropped a kiss on her parted lips before turning back to Cash with fury in his eyes.

Cash must have seen the anger in his eyes, too, because he took a deep breath and tilted his chin in challenge. "I won't apologize, Doc. I did what was necessary."

"You tried to kill my wife," Thomas said in a voice that would have formed icicles in the desert.

"Hey! Not your wife yet, buddy!" KJ protested, but Bryson sent her a quelling look.

"My soon to be wife, whatever. You tried to get her killed."

Cash shook his head violently. "No, man. I wasn't trying to get her killed, I was trying to save your life. There was no other way. Please understand. KJ has forgiven me, why can't you and Bryson?"

"You betrayed me, Cash. You were willing to turn her over to be a sex slave, in order to save my mangy hide! Next time, if I'm meant to die, let me die, because I could never live without her," Thomas said, and KJ gasped at the passion that rolled off him as he met her eyes. "I love her."

KJ stood, but Thomas held one finger up, stopping her. Before she could say anything else, he turned and slammed his fist into Cash's jaw knocking the man backward to the floor. The sound ricocheted through the room, and was followed by her scream, and Cash's grunt of pain. She started to move forward, but Thomas snagged her around the waist, while Bryson moved to Cash's side and held his hand out.

Cash flinched backward. "You gonna take your turn next, Samuels?"

Bryson laughed. "Nope. I think Doc did a fine job. In fact it's exactly what I would have done if he hadn't gotten to it first."

Cash took Bryson's hand and climbed to his feet before turning back to Thomas. "I'm sorry, Doc, I had to do it."

"I know, Cash. That's why you're still breathing," Thomas said, pressing a kiss to the crown of KJ's head.

"You've got a hell of a punch there, Doc," Noah said from across the room. "Where did you learn to hit like that?

"Who would have thought he might have some value?" Luke growled under his breath, but Thomas ignored him.

"The boxing ring, actually. I didn't have much of a social life, but I spent a lot of time at the gym. Guess you boys will have to practice to be able to take me…"

Luke snorted his disagreement, while Noah just grinned back. Everyone but KJ laughed. "What the fuck? Is this some sort of male bonding ritual? We've all come within inches of death in the last couple days, and I for one am tired of the fighting." She spun on Thomas and poked him in the chest, her rage bubbling to get out. "You! You don't get to stay in wolf form when I'm worrying about you, and then just shift on a whim!" Turning her anger to Bryson she snapped, "And you knew! You knew he could shift, and you were just waiting for it! Didn't either of you two asshats think that I might like to know my mate was going to survive? I mated you, Doc! If you go, I go!"

Thomas and Bryson exchanged looks before turning back to her. Suddenly her world was upside down and all she could see was Bryson's tight ass in front of her. Casually tossed over his shoulder she wailed and beat against his back in a rage. Just who did he think he was? She wouldn't be treated like this!

But she was being treated like this. Thomas held the door open as Bryson carried her outside and the other guys all told them goodnight. They were going to just take her away like none of her feelings even mattered. As angry as she was, she was also aroused. Having the choice taken away from her was a little bit of a turn on, and she clenched her thighs together when Bryson slapped her ass.

"No more, ice. You've said your piece. We're going back to the cabin and finishing the mating ritual, so we can go back to your den as an official triad. If you don't want your ass to be red you had better chill out." Bryson's voice rumbled through her body, and her nipples perked up at his threat.

"Don't I get a choice?" She paused long enough to ask, but when he just laughed, she screamed again. Her fists hit everywhere she could reach, and she even bit into his fleshy ass through his jeans. His grunt of irritation was the only response she got, and Thomas remained silent at their side.

"Aren't you going to stop him, Doc?" Turning her eyes up to him, she forced tears to fill them, knowing that Thomas hated seeing her cry.

A slow wicked grin that made her pussy drip spread across his face, and he laughed as his eyes took on a telltale glow. "Hell no. I like watching him spank you, and I fully intend on getting a few licks in myself, right before I fuck your ass."

Her breath caught in her throat and she choked on whatever words she might have said. He wanted to fuck her ass? Did that mean that Bryson would fuck her pussy? Did she even want that? Questions raced through her mind, and she struggled to keep from moaning at the rising heat in her blood.

"Hell, Doc. If we'd have known that threatening to fuck her ass would shut her up I would have started with that instead of 'Hi, I'm Bryson, your mate.'"

"You're a jerk."

"Yep, and you're horny. I can smell you from here, peaches. Now hush, so we can get to the good part faster."

~

Bryson carried KJ all the way into Rudy's old cabin where he set her down just inside the living room. The dining room table sat to their right, and it looked like the perfect height for what he had planned. When she stood upright on her feet again, he spun her quickly toward the wooden tabletop, and pushed her down until her chest was pressed to the top of it.

"Perfect," Thomas said softly as he followed them in and saw what Bryson had done.

"I think so. Now, would you like the honors, or should I go first."

KJ was growling low in her throat, but the burst of female arousal in the air told him that their little act was turning her on like crazy. She might have been cussing them under her breath, but her hips were cocked so her ass was presented to them neatly. He ran one hand over the denim covered curves gently while the other hand held both of her arms behind her back so she couldn't move.

"These have to go first, peaches." With that he shifted enough to have his claws pop through the skin, and he cut through the denim, careful not to cut her pale soft skin. It was like opening a delicious present as he pulled the material away from her body, leaving her completely bared to their eyes. He loved that she didn't bother with panties.

Thomas moved to his side, and ran his own hand over KJ's rump, too. She couldn't keep from moaning as they both gently caressed her back, butt, and thighs. As her muscles relaxed, Bryson felt his muscles harden. His cock was beating against his zipper like a hungry animal smelling its prey.

He pushed two fingers between her swollen pussy lips and groaned out loud when her body clenched down on him. She was so soft and hot that he nearly came in his jeans. Looking at Thomas's clenched jaw and large erection was like looking in a mirror. To be a man of his word he had to spank her first, but damn he wanted to sink into her until she was choking on him. Thomas beat him to the punch so to speak, when he brought his hand down on the fleshy part of her ass with a loud crack. She jumped and arched up off the table but didn't protest.

Her pussy approved, that was for sure. Bryson only debated for about two seconds before he dropped to his knees, releasing her arms, and gripping her hips. He pressed his face into her dripping cunt and licked her from top to bottom and back. She tasted musky and sweet at the same time, and when she gasped and whimpered his cock throbbed again.

Focusing on her clit, he heard Thomas spank her ass again, and then was treated to a tongue full of cream. It took everything he had not to beg Thomas to spank her again, but he couldn't figure out how to say it without it sounding creepy, so he just waited patiently for him to get on with it. They began a back and forth system of a slap or two and then a moment of clit worship, seeming to simultaneously agree that KJ was going to be the first one to come in this trio tonight.

He used his tongue like a finger, directing the pressure around her sensitive opening, and then just barely in before he flicked it back and forth. She squealed and then he heard the begging start.

"Please! Doc, please! Bryson, oh my God!" Over and over she repeated their names and begged for release until Thomas finally slid both hands down to grab her pink ass cheeks and spread them wide open for Bryson.

Bryson took advantage of the assistance and slowly rimmed her tiny rosebud. That did it. She shot up off the table against his mouth and came like a faucet. Her juices ran all over his chin and cheeks, while her ass muscles clenched around his face. He stopped moving long enough for her to catch her breath, and then he stood, and moved around to where her face was so he could take her mouth in a hot kiss. She moaned against his lips and tangled their tongues, and he wondered what she thought of her own flavor. Breaking free of her, he watched as Thomas began to rub his cock in the crease of her ass.

"Bry, grab the olive oil, and toss me that spoon right there." The suggestion burst in Bryson's brain like a firework, even as KJ spoke.

"What the hell? Are you fixing a meal or fucking?"

Thomas growled back at her, which seemed to shut her up

temporarily. "I'm going to fuck you, little one, but I refuse to hurt you. Now be quiet, or you won't get to come again all night long."

KJ and Bryson both let out matching grumbles of protest, but the fire in Thomas's eyes told Bryson that he was deadly serious.

Thomas stared at KJ's pink asshole and it winked back at him. She was anxious, but excited, or she would have been fighting like hell to get away from him. His mate wasn't a weak woman, and she wouldn't just lie there if she didn't want to.

Bryson handed him the olive oil and placed the wooden spoon on the arch of KJ's back. She squirmed at the foreign touch but calmed when Bryson tangled his fingers into her hair, and directed her face to his open fly. Thomas watched for a moment as KJ tongued her mate before opening her jaws and swallowing him down. That was a priceless moment. He envied Bryson, but he remained focused on his end goal.

Taking the wooden spoon in his hand, he landed it right in the center of her pretty pink ass cheeks, making her jump. The pretty oval red spot it left made his mouth water, so he did it again on another soft part of her ass cheek. He noticed after the third time that her hips were squirming, and he realized that she was trying to grind her clit against the edge of the table.

"No, you don't, little one. You're not coming again until you're full of cock." His voice sounded deeper and more raspy than usual as he tugged her hips back a little bit, taking the table away from her hot little clit.

"I think she likes the spoon, Tommy-boy!" Bryson said through clenched teeth, and they both grinned.

"I think she likes the spanking. I can't wait to show her how many things we can turn into a paddle. Just think, little one, we have the rest of our lives to fuck, and love, and Bry and I will have no problem spanking you when you get crazy."

She dropped Bryson's cock, and glared over her shoulder. "We'll just see about that, Doc."

Thomas laughed at her challenge, and paddled her again with the spoon, drawing a moan of pleasure from her, and Bryson rubbed his cock over her mouth. The sight of pre-cum on her swollen lips was divine, but he had his own mission.

He had an asshole to fuck.

Another brief thought crossed his mind, and he froze. His eyes shot to Bryson, who looked up at him in confusion. "What's wrong?"

Everyone froze as Thomas flushed guiltily. "I just realized that if I fuck her ass, then it means that I've taken both of her virginities. That seems pretty unfair."

Bryson's laughter barked out of him, and he groaned when KJ let his cock fall from her mouth again. "So, what, you want to leave me a virgin?"

"Not on your life, little one. I want to give Bry the chance to fuck your ass first." Thomas forced himself to take a step backward, secretly hoping that Bryson would decline. If he didn't get his cock inside of her soon, it was going to explode all over her.

Bryson hesitated until KJ slid her hand down to his balls, and cupped them, rolling them around in her palm. "No, Tom, it's all good. Peaches is giving her virginity to both of us, even if it's your cock leading the way. Fuck her, man, before I die here. I don't want to come until I'm balls deep inside of her."

"Thank God!"

Thomas moved like lightning to spill olive oil down the split of KJ's ass. She jerked and twitched but stayed in position for him. He ran his finger over the small opening, lovingly caressing it before pressing just the tip of his finger in. She let out a small grunt, but the muscles relaxed after a moment and he pushed his finger in fully. When she let out a sigh around Bryson's cock, Thomas knew he had her interested. Exchanging a mental fist bump with Bryson over her back, he slid a second finger in. She clenched on him, and he gritted his teeth to maintain slow, even pressure on her.

Thrusting his fingers in a gentle steady rhythm, he was able to convince her body to accept three of his fingers before long, and his cock ached for release. She had relaxed all her muscles in her jaw, and Bryson had her hair wrapped around his fist, while he pushed in and out of her mouth. His eyes were focused on what Thomas was doing though. It wouldn't be long before Bryson got his cock up her ass too.

This moment seemed surreal and spectacular at the same moment. He was greeting his destiny with open arms and a hard cock. A new voice in his head was growling and kept repeating the word *Mate* over and over. Knowing it was his new alter ego didn't make it any less unsettling, but right now, he was willing to just let the wolf instincts lead the way.

Pressing his aching dick against her tight asshole, he coated the shaft with olive oil, and directed it to heaven. She opened slowly to him and the tight ring of muscles was strangling his cock. She whimpered and clenched a couple times.

"Push back against him, peaches. Let him in," Bryson crooned to her, as he continued to fuck her face.

She obeyed his instructions and before long, Thomas was fully seated deep within her dark channel. It was pure bliss. The heat scorched him, and he struggled to take a deep breath. He had to keep control, or he was going to blow his load with the first thrust.

Gripping her hips in his hands, he marveled at how tiny she seemed when she was underneath him. The view from here was magnificent. From the tumble of blonde hair that scattered messily over her shoulders and down the strong line of her back, to the curve of her waist that spread into perfectly rounded hips made just for holding.

A slow retreat drew a growl from his throat that surprised him but seemed to turn her on. As he pushed back into his private paradise, he felt the new being in his body taking over, and he began to thrust into her more earnestly, fucking into her ass as Bryson pushed into her throat. She really was full of cock.

The rhythm was as old as time, but it felt brand-new. His body seemed tighter, hotter, and more needy than it ever had, and the voice of his wolf was screaming in his head to claim their mate. When Bryson pulled out of her mouth, gripping his cock tightly to keep from coming, Thomas knew it was time. Curving his body over her back so his chest pressed against her spine, he licked the tendon that arched gracefully from her shoulder to her neck, and then sunk his teeth into her.

This was the claiming that always should have been. Even if the first bite had saved his life, this one the one that would link them for eternity.

KJ's blood was on his tongue as he came deep inside her body, and she shattered underneath him. Her body convulsed around his cock, and her head thrashed wildly. Something seemed to pass through them, linking them to each other, and oddly enough, to Bryson as well, who held his now cum-covered cock in his hand, and watched them through droopy green eyes.

For several moments they remained locked together, his cock in her ass, and his lips pressed against her mating mark. It made his wolf excited to know that anyone she came across would see that mark and know who she belonged to for the rest of their lives. Talk about a hell of an ego boost.

"Don't you ever try to fucking die on me again, Doc." Her voice sounded slightly foggy, but her words were filled with the fear and pain that she had experienced.

Thomas's heart ached to fix it, but he knew that without that terrible moment in time, the likelihood of them seeing this perfect moment was slim. "I don't regret it, little one, and I would do it again, but I'll try my damnedest to stay out of trouble from now on. Because you asked so nicely."

"Good, now get off me, you weigh a ton!" She giggled as she spoke, and Thomas laughed too. He loved it that she seemed to be playful after sex. The emotional bond was growing as quickly as the physical bond, and it was everything he had ever hoped for from his future wife.

Standing up, he turned back to Bryson. "What happened, Rambo?"

"Fuck you. That was seriously hot, and she has the mouth of a goddess. I came the minute you claimed her. I swear to God I could feel it in my nut sack," Bryson said, looking slightly chagrined.

"Aww, poor baby. Let's take a shower and see about finishing this claiming stuff up. Do you think you can rise to the occasion?" KJ said, standing up on wobbly legs, and wrapping her arms around Bryson when he moved to her side.

"With you naked in the shower, there isn't a chance in hell I would fall down on the job. Move those gorgeous legs of yours, my wolf is dying to feel your teeth." Bryson nudged her toward the hallway, and the three of them made their way into the bathroom.

KJ felt Thomas's wolf already. It was there in her head and in her heart. She had claimed him. Their mating was complete, well, almost. Her heart told her that she needed Bryson too if she was ever going to be satisfied.

Moving quickly under the water, KJ sighed with pleasure when her two mates followed her, and began rubbing at her body, cleaning away the olive oil and sex that coated her skin. Thomas took her mouth in a passionate kiss that seemed to suck all her brain power away before he spun her around to face Bryson.

Bryson's trademark cheeky grin made her giggle, as he tweaked her nipples and then captured her mouth. His tongue quickly found its way between her lips and teased her. Caressing her teeth and tongue and pretty much every corner and crevice it could reach. The whole time, Thomas continued to wash her body with a washcloth and a bar of soap, cleaning the residue of their time together, so she could have her moment with Bryson.

She rubbed against Bryson's muscular chest, dancing her nipples over his skin, and shivering when it sent little lightning bolts to her clit.

After the last two knock-your-socks-off orgasms, she just couldn't imagine being turned on again so fast, but her slit was dripping again already.

"Bryson?"

"Yeah, baby?"

"I want you."

Those three little words seemed to just knock the breath out of his lungs, and his gorgeous green eyes darkened. His nostrils flared, and he licked his lips. "That's the nicest thing you've ever said to me, peaches."

She gripped his thickening cock in her hand and began stroking it gently trying to find a rhythm as he hardened against her palm. He reached out and wrapped one of his large hands around hers to direct her, and let his head fall back as she followed his direction.

Thomas was on his knees behind her, sliding the washcloth up between her legs, and massaging her pussy gently until she was moaning. Bryson pinched her nipple at the same time as Thomas shoved two fingers up her aching channel, and she gasped, her eyes meeting Bryson's.

Bryson glanced over her shoulder, and Thomas pulled away from her. Lifting her easily, Bryson put her back against the cold tile of the shower stall, and thrust his cock deep into her pussy. There was no gentleness at this point, it was just raw hard fucking, finding release in the most primal way possible. KJ loved it. She heard her own voice crying out with every slam of Bryson's hips, and she dug her fingernails into the tight muscles of his biceps, while her heels dug into his ass.

Again and again he slammed his cock into her body, and she felt like she wanted to absorb him until he was a part of her. That thought had barely crossed her mind when her wolf took over, and she bit down hard on his shoulder. The link formed, and later she would swear that she heard a definitive click as the world fell into place for the three of them. She heard Thomas growl and Bryson groan, as his soul met hers and they mated. It was complete.

With a sigh she released him and fell over the cliff to her own orgasm. Her eyes drifted closed on the sight of Thomas coming all over his own hand, with his head thrown back in ecstasy, and his mouth slightly open calling her name, while Bryson's cum filled her womb.

The two men must have washed her clean after she passed out because she woke up snuggled in between them in the bed and sweating like a pig in the desert. Shoving at Thomas's shoulder, she pushed back with her ass against Bryson, trying to give herself a little bit of breathing room. Cuddling was great most of the time, but these two men were like her own personal space heaters.

"What's wrong, peaches?" Bryson rumbled from behind her, clamping his hand over her bare belly and pulling her back against him tightly.

She huffed and tried to move again. "I'm trying to avoid dying of heat exhaustion, but you two aren't allowing it."

Thomas chuckled, and scooted over a little, trying to give her some space. "Oh yeah, because we wouldn't want you to pass out on us, huh?"

Smacking his chest hard enough to make her hand sting, she rose up between them onto her knees. They looked up at her and she grinned when two sets of eyes zeroed in on her naked breasts. She couldn't deny the power they had over her. Her nipples perked right up just knowing that they had their undivided attention.

Thomas and Bryson were so different, and yet somehow the three of them interlocked into a neat little package. Like three puzzle pieces meant to be together, but unsure until now how they fit. Bryson's light to Thomas's dark made her stomach clench with desire.

If only they knew how much of her heart, body, and soul they already owned. Flushing at her own thoughts, she tried to go for sarcasm. "I happen to be the only one here who had more than two orgasms. I think I deserve the rest."

"Poor, ice. Having to suffer through multiple orgasms to keep her mates content," Bryson said with a snort of derision.

"One of these days, you two will regret teasing me so much." She knew that her lip stuck out in a pout, but she had to know how much control she had over them.

Thomas immediately lifted her up until she was straddling his hips, and Bryson landed a sharp smack on her ass cheeks. "I wouldn't suggest reverting to threats, little one. We won't take kindly to them. Now, if you want to be fucked, all you had to do was ask. Bryson grab the lotion out of the bathroom. I saw some on the counter."

KJ narrowed her eyes at Thomas and glared at him. "Just what do you think you're doing, Mr. Jameson?"

He rocked his hips up at the same time as he pushed her down, so his cock split her pussy lips and settled perfectly in the seam of her sex against her clit. Moisture flooded her, dripping all over his cock, and making him grin.

"Not I, little one, we. We are going to fulfill one of your darkest fantasies." He spoke in a low deep voice that rattled her bones. When she felt the cold creamy lotion hit her asshole she jumped and threw a surprised glance over her shoulder at Bryson, who just grinned back wickedly. "Bend forward, and put your hands on my shoulders, love."

She hesitated, but the tightness of Thomas's jaw muscles warned her not to push him too far, and she did as he asked. Once she was in position, she felt Bryson's finger easing into her tight asshole. Her breath caught in her throat and she tried to focus on relaxing as he pressed a second finger into her.

"That's so beautiful," Bryson said in a husky tight voice as he watched his fingers slipping and sliding into her. She wanted to look at him, but she was caught in Thomas's dark gaze. His hands reached up to cup her face, and he took her mouth in a fierce battle of kiss control. She nipped at him, while he sucked her bottom lip into his mouth, and fenced with her tongue. It distracted her completely, and before she knew it, Bryson's cock was pushing into her dark passage. It burned, but less so than the first time with Thomas, and she adjusted quickly.

Once he was seated inside of her, he wrapped one arm around her waist, lifting her up and back, while Thomas grabbed his cock and pointed it at her dripping opening.

"You go next, Doc, just keep your aim true," Bryson said, catching KJ off guard and making her laugh, which in turn made him groan. "Shit, baby, don't laugh or I'll blow!"

Thomas growled. "Would you just shut up, Bry? I'm trying to fuck our woman, and you're still cracking jokes."

Bryson bit KJ's earlobe and whispered, "Don't mind him, he's just jealous that I'm in your ass and he's not. He'll get over it when he gets inside of you."

She cried out when Thomas pushed up into her pussy as Bryson lowered her down. The fullness was overwhelming. She felt like she was being split in two, but in a good way. Her pussy was stretched snuggly around Thomas's cock, while Bryson gently retreated from her ass. The two men began rocking in time with each other very slowly, and she felt a burning building in her belly.

This was what a ménage meant. She was being fucked thoroughly by her mates. Not her boyfriends, but her mates. The two men that she would be with forever and ever. It made the moment even more sentimental to her, and she felt tears leak from her eyes. Thomas frowned up at her, and she gave him a halfhearted smile of reassurance.

It didn't take long for the two men to bring her to the edge of the mountain again, and before she knew it she was pinned between two sated men, full of cum and tingling all over. It was magnificent, and she couldn't wait to do it again.

CHAPTER THIRTEEN

*T*he next morning was tense and awkward as everyone loaded into the vans. The only tussle seemed to be over which van Luke would ride in, as his coldness toward Thomas still hadn't eased. KJ couldn't put her finger on what Luke's problem was, but she was determined to address it as soon as they were back to the den. A phone call to Devin this morning filled them in on the Diego Pack's Alpha battle, and it sounded as though there had been plenty of drama back at the den while they were gone. Rafe and Ryley were anxious to get home to Shandi, and to face-off with Whitney's new mates.

The ride kicked off full of starts and stops as they had children with them this time. Who knew that Axel had trouble with motion sickness? One van now had the stomach-turning odor of vomit.

Pressed between her mates, KJ found the ride both arousing and frustrating at the same time. She couldn't act on her physical desire to fuck her men, and she couldn't release the physical tension by taking a run. Her wolf was going nuts.

To top it all off, no one had seen or heard from any of the Kaplan wolves since the battle. Everyone was on edge wondering if they would back off now that they had taken such a large loss of life, or if they were just regrouping. Being on the verge of war really didn't do good things to people's mental state, so they were all grumpy and exhausted.

Finally, Rafe had had enough of the griping and complaining, and he pulled into a rest stop about halfway home. "Everyone take a run, or get something to eat, or just get out of the vehicles. We need a break. Axel needs to stop moving for a while, and I think Tasha needs a little quiet time. Just be back here in two hours." He ran a hand through his blond hair in frustration, and then moved quickly to Axel's side as the boy held his arms up asking for a hug.

They were parked in front of the gas station portion of the rest stop. A small walking park was to their left, and a fast food restaurant was to the right. Behind the building was a wooded area, and KJ perked up. Turning to Thomas, she smiled. "Hey, Doc, do you want to go *rest?*"

It took Thomas a minute, but Bryson caught on immediately and began dragging her back behind the gas station toward the wooded area. She wrinkled her nose as they passed a dingy trash dumpster and a pickup truck that had seen better days. The trio walked about two hundred feet into the woods before Bryson stopped and jerked her against his body.

"I've missed holding you, peaches," he grumbled as he pressed hot kisses against her mouth, jaw, and throat.

She laughed and shivered as Thomas pressed against her backside. "You've been holding me the whole time we've been driving."

"Yeah, but not the way I *want* to hold you." He gripped her hips and lifted her until her legs wrapped around his waist. She locked her ankles and held onto his shoulders while Thomas cupped her ass cheeks.

"Rambo, you better stop talking so much and get your clothes off." Running her tongue over his Adam's apple, she scraped the skin with her canine teeth, and grinned when he groaned.

Thomas massaged her ass through her jeans, and she turned to meet his mouth in a deep kiss. When they both pulled back, she tipped her head, so it was resting against his chest, while she remained wrapped in Bryson's arms.

"If Bry can't do the job, little one, I have wood hard enough to pound nails right now." Thomas growled against her ear and she moaned.

"Fuck you, dickwad. I can take care of her. I bet I can make her scream louder than you can," Bryson said, releasing one hand from her hip now that she was supported against Thomas too, and moved it to her swollen breast. She automatically thrust up into his hand, hoping that he would pinch and pull her nipples the way she liked him to. When he complied with her unspoken request, she growled low in her throat, and her pussy creamed, scenting the air with her arousal.

"Challenge accepted, polar-boy. I'll even let you go first." Thomas pressed another kiss to the side of her neck, just nicking her skin with his teeth enough to make her squirm against Bryson, and then he stepped away from them. She watched him adjust his hard cock down the thigh of his jeans and then cross his arms tightly over his chest. Her mouth watered at the sight of that thick piece of meat just begging for release. As much as she liked that they were going to bring her to screaming orgasms, she was a little disappointed that it wouldn't be at the same time.

Bryson managed to release her long enough to strip her jeans down to her ankles, and spin her to face a wide tree. Instinctively she knew he wanted her to bend over, and she braced herself against the rough tree bark. His fingers teased into her opening, and she spread her ankles as wide as possible to give him room. Expertly, he brought her to the edge of climax, and she was gasping and pleading for release when he finally thrust his cock into her.

She rocked forward into the tree, feeling the wood support her weight as Bryson lifted her off her feet and held her by the hips, plowing his cock deep into her cunt. Spasms rippled through her inner vagina and she started to tremble. Reaching around her, Bryson gripped her clit between his thumb and forefinger and squeezed, just hard enough to make her scream his name, and come all over his hand

and cock. Once he knew that she was finished, he pumped his own release into her, and pressed kisses to her spine.

"Perfection, peaches. You are absolute perfection. You didn't even hesitate about having sex out here in the open where just anyone could interrupt us." Bryson's words brought reality crashing down around her, and she froze, her gaze darting around for an invisible intruder.

When he realized what made her tense up, Bryson chuckled. "There is no one here, ice, stand down."

"Someone could have watched us!" she gasped in fear and arousal. She couldn't have told him which emotion was stronger at the moment.

"That's the beauty of it, little one. Anyone could be watching us fuck our mate to mind-blowing orgasms, and the whole time they will envy Bryson and I our positions."

She gave him her best stink eye, and growled. "Are you saying you want strangers to want to have sex with me?"

Thomas sighed. "No, love. I'm saying that I'm proud of the mate I have, and I want other men to be jealous of the fact that I'm with her and they are not. Now stop talking before we run out of time, little one."

He tipped her face and kissed her before dropping to his knees to help her remove her shoes and jeans. Once she was bare from the waist down, he pressed a kiss to her pubic bone, just above her pussy. The look on his face was very nearly reverent, and it warmed her heart.

Thomas stood, and lifted her up in the same position Bryson had held her earlier. Her legs wound around his waist; her arms tight around his neck. The display of strength didn't go unnoticed by her, when he sat her down on his hard cock, and she felt the earth spin. From this angle there wasn't a spot in her pussy that he couldn't reach. Every time he lifted her and dropped her, her clit rubbed against him and she let out a small cry.

"Thomas, please!"

"In a minute, little one, first you have to scream for me."

The next thing she knew, his fingers were wrapped in her hair, forcing her head backward so he could reach her neck and collarbone. Just when her body started to clench on him and shudder with an orgasm, he bit down on her mating mark, and she screamed out his name. Nothing could have ruined the moment.

Hell, at this point a reporter from the tabloids with a telephoto lens wouldn't have upset her, and she rocked against Thomas until the waves of release subsided for both of them.

"Fuck, Doc. You just had to ruin my fun," Bryson grumbled from beside them. He looked ridiculously disappointed, and KJ couldn't resist a quick jab.

"I can't help it if he knows just the right buttons to push," she said as she climbed off her mate, and began to redress.

"Next time, I'll have the remote control, and I'll pick which buttons we push," he said with a chuckle in her ear, and a kiss on her temple.

Absolute perfection. This moment in time was just that.

Hours of driving and a dozen rest stops later, KJ saw the lights of Kansas City to their north as they turned off the highway onto the road into the den. The sun had only been up for a few hours, and most of the wolves in the van she rode in were sleeping. She was settled against Thomas, with his arm hanging over her shoulder, and her legs were draped over Bryson's lap. Bryson slept deeply, while Thomas just dozed, but KJ couldn't seem to quiet her mind as she entered the next phase of her life.

First things first, Tasha's surgery had to happen as quickly as possible, so she had a fighting chance. Thomas had already spoken with Caroline, who was going to have a room set up and the tools needed to do the job. Calling in a few favors, Tina and Thomas were able to secure the items they would need, but KJ was still scared. Surgery was a big deal, made even bigger by the fact that they weren't doing it in a real hospital. She trusted Thomas, but this was her mother, and right now her entire existence rested on him, Caroline, and Tina. It was terrifying for her, how must it be for her mother?

The van slid to a stop in front of the Alpha cabin, and KJ sat up ready to bolt out the door. Thomas's hand on her shoulder stopped her.

"You can't run yet, little one. We have a few things to clear up with the Alpha before you can stretch. When we're finished you and Bry can go for a long run with the rest of the pack while I fix your mom."

She nodded, blinking back tears. He was trying to make her feel better about the surgery, but he had been completely honest about the risks. Even if the surgery was successful and Tasha survived it, she still had a rough road ahead of her.

Devin and Damon Gray stood with Caroline on the porch of their cabin waiting as everyone unloaded. Rafe carried a wilted-looking Axel, while Ryley had his arms full of Jordan, and Shandi came running the moment she laid eyes on them. KJ watched in awe as the new little family formed, and Axel went right into Shandi's arms.

Shandi rocked the child, as tears spilled down her cheeks, and Rafe kissed her gently. Ryley followed suit, but his kiss met her forehead because her lips were on little Jordan's cheek. She was going to make a fantastic mother.

Relieved to see some positive coming from the devastating grief that they all still shared, she watched as the members of her family were introduced to the members of the Gray Pack. The only one missing was Whitney, and oddly enough there were no Diego Pack members present even though the air still held their scent.

Cash moved up to KJ and Bryson who lingered near the van with Thomas, and he threw an arm over each of them. His normally beautiful face was marred by the black and blue bruise across his lower jaw from Thomas's sense of justice, but his grin was full of mischief.

"Welcome home, guys! We managed to get you here, now we can all relax and let loose. I'm seeing a visit to Rustler's in our near future!" Cash said.

"What is Rustler's?" Bryson asked.

"Only the best bar in town with the best singer on stage," Cash answered.

"It's the bar that Cash sings at." Owen filled in the blanks as the Alpha twins came over to meet them.

"KJ, it's good to see you again. I hear you have some news," Damon said eyeing Bryson curiously.

"Bryson Samuels, this is Damon Gray and his brother Devin. Devin is the Alpha of the Gray Pack." KJ introduced them, and Bryson shook their hands. Thomas moved up behind her and kissed the top of her head.

"Little one, I'm taking your mother in to get her settled. We have to do the surgery soon, but you'll have time to talk with her first. I love you."

"I love you too, Doc. We'll be in soon."

Damon and Devin watched Thomas as he moved to help Graham get Tasha from the van and they led her in the house. When they were out of view, Devin turned back to Bryson.

"So you're a Kaplan?"

Bryson shook his head. "I *was* a Kaplan, right now my only allegiance is to my mate and my partner. Where they go, I go."

Devin cocked his head and looked Bryson over. "What level?"

"Omega."

Surprise lit Devin's face. "Really? I would have thought Beta."

"No, in the Kaplan Pack no one who isn't related to Evan Kaplan makes Beta level. We're all just muscle and based on how they left my fellow Omegas dead in Quiver Creek I would say we were just armor to protect Nico's tender ass."

Damon let out a low whistle. "I heard you guys had a tough time up there. Have you had any trouble on the trip back?"

"No, not a sound out of them since the battle, but it's not over."

KJ swung her eyes to stare at Bryson in shock. Surely it was over. There was no way Nicolas Kaplan would be stupid enough to show up here, right?

"You think they will attack us here?" she asked in a high-pitched voice that trembled with anxiety.

Bryson nodded. "Yes, I do. Nicolas won't stop until he's dead, peaches." He met Devin's steady gaze. "If you'll have me, I would like to pledge my allegiance to you and your pack. My mate's family is here, and I have no loyalty in my heart for Evan or Nicolas at this point."

"I will gladly accept it. You are welcome here, but I don't have an Omega position for you," Devin said with a frown. Bryson's face fell, and KJ's heart followed it. What would they do if Bryson couldn't help the pack? "I think you would serve us better as a Beta wolf, but you'll have to prove yourself. Let's call it a trial run. At the moment we are a little overwhelmed with people, as the Diego Pack is still here. They will be leaving soon."

"And taking my little sister with them!" Liam snarled from behind KJ, and she frowned at him.

"What's happened?"

"Whitney seems to have lost her mind and decided that two of those animals are her mates. Ridiculous," Liam said. His pierced eyebrow arched in irritation, and the muscles of his arms bunched with frustration as he shifted in place.

"Shut up, hotshot. Whitney knows what's best for Whitney, and you will stay out of it." Liam's mate, Tina stepped up to his side, and she hugged KJ. "Welcome home. I'm glad to hear that I'm at least getting a new sister now that the one I thought I had is moving to Chicago with her new pack."

KJ hugged the slim brunette back and swallowed hard against the emotions threatening to overwhelm her. "Thank you, Tina."

"Well at least one female around here was smart enough to pick males of her species to mate with."

The words pierced KJ's heart, and she gasped in shock. Several growls of anger sounded, as she spun to face Luke who leaned against the van sulking like a child.

"What the hell is your problem, Luke?" she snapped.

"I'm sick of seeing wolves' mating with humans. It's bad enough we have to be secretive and hide what we really are from humans every day, why the fuck should we be bringing them into our pack?" Luke's voice dripped acid, and his hazel eyes flashed with pent up rage.

"Luke, I didn't choose to mate a human. You know that. Fate put me with Thomas. Just like it brought Bryson into my life," KJ said, trying to control her temper before her wolf attacked Luke.

"Yeah, sure. Fuck Fate." Luke pushed off the van and headed into the woods, leaving behind a stunned and furious pack of wolves behind.

"What the hell was that?" Tina asked.

Owen sighed. "All I know is he's been acting like an ass ever since he realized KJ was mating Thomas. I don't know what's triggering it, but that kid has some serious anger issues."

Devin looked furious. "I'll handle Luke. No member of my pack will treat any other member like that. We fight too much adversity already, we don't need to be fighting ourselves from within. Now, we had better get inside and get Tasha taken care of. Later tonight I'm sure there will be time for you all to meet the Diego Pack."

Thomas watched as KJ and her brothers hugged Tasha one more time before surgery. Caroline stood nearby with her hand stroking her rounded belly and tears in her eyes. His anxiety was high. He knew how close to death Tasha was, but he couldn't seem to make her children understand that. Graham met his eyes, and Thomas knew that *he* at least comprehended the gravity of the circumstances.

How would he be able to tell KJ that he failed if Tasha died under his hand? He loved her and he would do anything within in his power to make her happy, but at this point, he didn't know if this was one of those things or not.

Turning to Tina, he nodded, and she began the process of herding Tasha away from her children and into the office that they had set up for surgery. Thomas headed in the opposite direction to scrub up. He was nervous about doing this procedure in this location and with just the bare bones as far as tools went, but he had no other choice. Sure, he could refuse to do it, but then Tasha would refuse the surgery at all, and he would have to watch her die knowing that it was his decision not to try.

He scrubbed his hands until they were raw and pink before Tina stepped in covered in a mask and gown. Her eyes were the only thing he could see of her face, and they reflected his own tension.

"You ready for this, Tommy?" she asked, cocking her head as she helped him into a pair of gloves.

"I have to be, Tink. Is she ready?"

Tina nodded. "Caro has her down for the count. Thank God Devin bought that disaster kit last summer. The battery-powered respirator is the only reason we're able to do this here."

"Were you able to get a heart monitor, too?"

She nodded, and grinned, "Of course! I just charmed my way through a few friends at St. Leo's. We got all the sterilization equipment and the oxygen tank from there, too."

"You realize that is ridiculously illegal, right?" Thomas asked.

"That's where the rush of excitement comes in. We're saving her life, Tommy. Now, let's get to it before we lose our window of opportunity."

Thomas led the way back into the office where Tasha lay on a table that had been raised about eight inches to make it high enough for him to reach. Caroline sat next to her, monitoring her blood pressure, pulse, and the oxygen tank. Comforted by the sound of the oxygen tank's hiss, he moved with purpose directly to his patient's side without really paying any attention to Caroline. "Okay, do we have everything?"

"Don't move," Caroline whispered, and Thomas's eyes shot up to hers. She was pale faced, and her hands trembled on her lap as she stared over his shoulder. Thomas swallowed hard, and suddenly he caught a familiar scent in his nose.

Nicolas Kaplan.

Turning slowly, he found himself face-to-face again with the over-sized man. His long white hair was pin straight, but his eyes were as wild as the overgrown beard on his jaw. He held Tina by the throat up on her toes, squeezing hard enough she couldn't have sounded the alarm, but not tight enough to really hurt her. "Hello again, human... or should I say, wolf? Tell me, how does a human go about shifting into a werewolf?"

"What do you want, Nicolas?"

"I heard a vicious rumor that you have mated with my intended, but I'm sure it's just a rumor, right?"

"I am mated to KJ."

"Well damn the luck. I'm going to have to kill you now."

Thomas's eyes shot to Tina's, and back to Nicolas's. "If you kill me, it will kill her."

Nicolas laughed. "No, see I already knew you had fucked my bride, and I know that my ex-Omega Bryson Samuels has mated her too. Once I finish with you, I intend to keep him just barely alive, and make him watch while I fuck the shit out of Katie Jo Whetstone."

"You won't make it out of the den alive." Thomas's mind was racing. He had to do something. His wolf was so loud in his brain that he was beginning to wonder if it was making noise out loud.

"Surely you don't believe I would come alone? Right now, my Omegas are ripping the rest of your pack to pieces. There will be nothing left of the Gray Pack but the empty cabins they once occu-pied." Kaplan's laugh had an eerie, hollow quality to it, and it sent butterflies fluttering in Thomas's stomach. He had to keep Nicolas talking until he figured out a plan to get out of this mess.

"All because of a gold mine that may or may not exist."

Nicolas's eyes narrowed. "Oh, it exists all right. Tasha knew where it was, but alas she won't be alive long enough to lead the way, so her daughter will have to do."

"KJ has never even met her grandfather, why do you think she knows where the gold mine is?"

The question seemed to stop Nicolas in his tracks. "It's a fortune in gold, and it's been willed to her, why wouldn't she know?"

"Like I said, she didn't have a relationship with her grandfather, so until you mentioned it to her, she didn't even know that there was a gold mine."

"Hmm…well that does change things a bit, doesn't it? I suppose I could just kill her and take whatever is hers based on her having no living heirs, or I could make you wake Tasha and drag her dying ass back to Alaska, hoping she would survive it—"

"Or I can slit your fucking throat you fucking asshole." Bryson's voice echoed viciously through the room, followed by a gurgle and the sound of air escaping lungs. Thomas wasn't sure if the sound came from Tina who was suddenly released, or from Nicolas, whose throat now gaped open. He watched in astonishment, as Bryson slid his knife into the wound, and held it there, staring straight into his ex-Alpha's eyes. "You can't shift with a knife in your throat, which means we get to watch you die a slow, painful death. Better start praying you bleed out fast."

Kaplan's eyes rolled up in his head, and his face drained of blood just before he slumped over Bryson's arm. Bryson jumped back letting the dead man fall to the ground and cursed.

"Fuck, that was supposed to take longer. Tell me, Tom, why is it that they die so much slower in the movies?"

Thomas laughed, and gave Bryson a one-armed hug. "Because man, they need the dramatic moment to keep the viewers happy. Well done. How did you know he was here?"

Bryson tapped his nose and then his temple. "Intuition first. I grew up watching Evan and Nicolas. I know all their tricks, and when I walked back through the hallway after everyone spread out, I caught his scent. And then I heard you in my head, praying that I would keep KJ safe. Dude, really? Like you even have to ask something like that? Of course, I would keep her safe."

Thomas shook his head at the reminder that wolf mates seem to be able to form a unique ability to hear each other's thoughts. What a weird weird world he had joined.

"Bryson, he said that his pack was here!" Caroline said from behind Thomas. He turned to the pregnant woman and took in her pale face.

"Take it easy, Caro. Stress isn't good for the babies. Bryson, you'll have to be our liaison, as we have a surgery to accomplish."

"You got it, Tommy-boy. Be right back." Bryson was gone before Thomas could say any more, and he turned back to Caroline and Tina.

"Are you two okay to do this?"

When they both nodded, Thomas had to force himself to push everything else out of his brain and focus on the patient in front of him. "Okay, let's re-sterilize everything, and get rid of the body. I'm not risking it when she's so close to death as it is."

The dead man lay on the floor behind him, his blood staining the once-pristine beige carpet, but not one of the three wolves felt remorse for him. What was done was done, and Nicolas Kaplan deserved what he got.

Tina and Thomas lifted Nicolas and drug him into the hallway, before returning to the bathroom to change their surgical gowns and rescrub. By the time they returned, Caroline had sanitized as much as possible, and had the new surgical tools waiting.

Taking one last deep breath to steady himself, Thomas let his training take over, and he went to work.

Bryson made it as far as the front lawn before he heard the laughter in the woods. Shifting into his wolf, he bounded in the direction of the noise only to find about twenty of his former pack members surrounded by fifty or so Gray and Diego Pack wolves. His old pack mates looked terrified, and his new pack mates looked pleased as hell. A shiver went through him as he wondered if the Diego Pack wolves had been informed that he was on the good side now. If not, this could get messy fast. Shifting back into his skin he moved closer to the circle, and Devin turned around to greet him.

"Ah, Bryson there you are. See, these gentlemen tell me that they are here on Gray Pack land in search of a lost wolf. Did you realize you were lost?" Devin asked with a grin.

Bryson relaxed when he realized that his new pack mates weren't going to turn on him or allow his old pack mates access to him. "I'm not lost, but I appreciate the thought. I didn't figure many of them even knew my name."

"Traitor!" someone yelled from the middle of the circled-up wolves.

"Traitor? Really? Just who exactly did I betray?" Bryson asked, forcing his face into a frown of curiosity. He still had Nicolas's blood all over his hands, and he knew they could smell it in the air. "The way I see it, with Nico dead, there isn't anyone left to give out commands, which means that I've betrayed no one."

"I would agree with that," Damon hollered back from across the group. "So boys, now that the worm has been removed from your apple, are you going to get the fuck off our land, or are we going to have to force you out."

"How do we know Nico is really dead?" The wolf speaking was a good wolf that had been loyal to his leader and wouldn't be happy without proof. Bryson held his hands out for inspection.

"I know you smell it. That's the scent of death, and it's all over my hands because I cut his throat myself. No one will threaten my mate and live to tell about it," Bryson said calmly. More than one of the Kaplan wolves shuddered at his threat, and they began to grumble to each other.

The pseudoleader turned and faced Bryson down for several moments before he nodded. "We'll go but let us take his body back home. If we don't his Alpha will never believe he's dead."

"Done," Devin said before Bryson could respond. "Cash, Noah,

Liam get the body and give it to them. If you're not at least ten miles from my land by sunset, we'll finish this the hard way."

With that, Devin turned and walked to Bryson's side, clapping him on the back. "So, you killed him?"

Bryson grinned. "Slit his throat before he could even blink."

"What kind of moron thinks he can sneak into a pack den?" The man who spoke was taller than Bryson, and broad as a barn. His dark hair, darker eyes, and golden skin coloring bespoke a Hispanic heritage. His accent confirmed it. Before Bryson could respond, a second man just barely shorter than the first stepped to his side.

"Is your pack always so dramatic, Gray?"

Devin laughed and shook his head. "Sure, has been lately."

"See what happens when you add women into the mix," Owen said with a shrug of his shoulders. All the men laughed, and the shorter of the new men pointed at him.

"Don't say that, you'll jinx yourself." He turned to Bryson and held out his hand. "Hello to you, Bryson Samuels, I'm Cadence Diego."

Bryson shook his hand and they all headed back to the Alpha cabin. The men chatted for a while on the front lawn, swapping stories of what had occurred both in Quiver Creek, and back at the Gray Pack den.

More than an hour later, Bryson suddenly caught KJ's scent and looked up to find Thomas and KJ on the porch wrapped in each other's arms.

"Looks like the surgery must have been a success," Damon said and everyone laughed. Bryson shot forward with a low growl, reaching his mates in record time.

"Well? How did it go?"

KJ turned teary eyes up to him, but her face was covered in a beautiful smile. "She made it through surgery!" Bryson swung her around in his arms with a laugh and hugged her tight.

"That's fantastic, peaches!"

"She's not out of the woods yet, but I was able to get the bullet and all the necrotic tissue that I could find. There was a lot of infection, but she shifted just a few minutes ago, so now we wait and hope her body heals itself." Thomas filled in everyone as they reached the porch.

"That's the second-best news I've heard all day," Devin said. "Nicolas Kaplan is dead. The Diego Pack challenge is completed, and Tasha made it through surgery. Shit, it's been a long week."

KJ looked up at Bryson and winked. "Yes, it has, and I'm thinking we should go to bed...to rest."

She took off into the woods, shifting into her beautiful, golden-colored wolf, and Thomas was only a second behind her, shifting into his large black wolf as he ran. Bryson watched them disappear in awe at the beauty of their pairing.

"Hey, man, I'm not one to give advice, but I would suggest you join them. Otherwise Doc is going to be getting all the good stuff," Noah said from behind Bryson, sending all the other men into roars of laughter.

Bryson hit the ground running to meet his mate and his partner. This life was a dream come true compared to the life he had before, and he intended to enjoy every moment of it.

THE END

WWW.LORIKINGBOOKS.COM

ABOUT THE AUTHOR

Lori King is the author of more than thirty Amazon best-selling romance novels, as well as a full-time wife and mother of three boys. Although she rarely has time to just enjoy feminine pursuits; at heart she is a hopeless romantic. She spends her days dreaming up Alpha men, and her nights telling their stories. An admitted TV and book junkie, she can be found relaxing with a steamy story, or binging in an entire season of some show online. She gives her parents all the credit for her unique sense of humor and acceptance of all forms of love. There are no two loves alike, but you can love more than one with your whole heart.

With the motto: Live, Laugh, and Love like today is your only chance, she will continue to write as long as you continue to read. Thank you for taking the time to indulge in a good Happily Ever After with her. Find out more about her current projects at http://lorikingbooks.com.

ALSO BY LORI KING

Crawley Creek Series

Contemporary Western/Small Town Suspense

Beginnings

Forget Me Knot

Rough Ride Romeo

Claiming His Cowgirl

Sunnyside Up

Hawke's Salvation

Handcuffed by Destiny

The Lawman's Lover

Paw Prints on Her Heart

Fetish & Fantasy

Contemporary BDSM

Watching Sin

Submission Dance

Mistress Hedonism

Masquerade

Surrender Series

Contemporary Western Ménage

Weekend Surrender

Flawless Surrender

Primal Surrender

Broken Surrender

Fantasy Surrender

The Gray Pack Series

Paranormal Suspense

Fire of the Wolf

Reflections of the Wolf

Legacy of the Wolf

Dreams of the Wolf

Caress of the Wolf

Honor of the Wolf

Apache Crossing

Sidney's Triple Shot

Sunset Point

Point of Seduction

Storm Corps

The Marine's Seduction

Pieced Together

Tempting Tanner

www.LoriKingBooks.com

EXCERPT FROM CARESS OF THE WOLF

The Gray Pack Book 5

There was barely a whisper of sound as wolves bled out of the forest onto the grassy bank of the lake that bordered Gray pack land. The first to shift had to be Devin, but he did so reluctantly. For a few precious moments while he was in his human skin, he would be exposed to wolves he didn't completely trust. As the leader, it was his duty, but as a man, it was his burden.

After forcing himself out of his furry form, he rose to his feet and broadened his stance, unflinching in his nudity beneath the gaze of ten strange wolves. Barely a breath passed before they all began to shift into their human forms, and then instead of wolves, he faced a pack of large muscular men.

"Devin Gray?" The man speaking was easily in the six foot four range, and he looked like a bruiser. He had broad shoulders that probably caused him as much difficulty buying shirts as they brought him women to his bed. Paired with black hair in a short military cut and dark Hispanic coloring, he was so unlike what Devin expected that he hesitated for a moment before nodding.

"Cadence Diego?" he asked, holding his hand out for the younger man.

The return handshake was firm, but not overly so. There seemed to be no animosity in the man's body language that he could surmise. His late enemy's son was significantly older than he had expected. "Yes, I'm Cadence, and this is my cousin Mateo Diego." Standing next to Cadence was a man of similar build, but instead of broad shoulders narrowing into a slim waist, Mateo was proportionately wider. He looked like a professional bodybuilder, and a shiver of apprehension skittered down Devin's spine as the man cautiously nodded to him.

Behind them stood a pair of older men, one Devin recognized immediately, and as their eyes met, he felt his lip curl up in disgust. "Rolando Asis."

"Gray." Rolando smirked back, obviously aware of Devin's disdain for him, but he didn't say anything further.

"Are we enemies, Devin Gray?" Cadence asked, looking pensive as he watched Devin and Rolando square off.

Devin shook his head. "Not necessarily, but the last time I met up with a Diego wolf we weren't exactly on a social outing. I'm sorry for your loss, Cadence, but I won't apologize for killing him."

"Bastard! You killed Barton because you want to take over the Diego pack. Admit it. That's what you've always wanted." Rolando's outburst surprised them all.

"Stop it, Rolando. You promised us all that you would be civil. I apologize for Rolando's outburst. He's still grieving." The oldest man there held out his hand to Devin. "Alastair Cooper. Thank you for allowing us to hold our contest here. I don't envy you the convincing you must have done with your pack to clear the path for it."

"That's where you're mistaken." Damon stepped forward to stand shoulder to shoulder with Devin as he, too, shook hands with the Diego pack wolves. "Dev doesn't have to ask permission. The Gray pack knows that he would never do anything to put them in harm's way. They stand behind their Alpha one hundred percent."

Cadence nodded. "However, it happened, we thank you. We assure you that we have come here in peace and friendship. As Alastair said,

Rolando has been grieving for my father. They were friends for many years, but I'm sure he will agree that it won't happen again."

The look on Rolando's face was nasty as he glared at Cadence, but he nodded after a few moments of tense silence. It was a good thing the Diego pack was going to be naming an Alpha soon. Devin figured whoever earned the title in the match would surely still have his work cut out for him with the rest of the pack.

Gesturing to his men to step forward, he named them off individually, ensuring that the werewolves in front of him knew how close he was to his Betas. They would see his knowledge of his team as a sign of strength. It was important that they knew who the leader was here.

"Now that we're all introduced, let's get you back to the den. We've set up a couple cabins. Unfortunately, for the moment we're short on space, so you'll have to bunk together. A situation came up for our pack after we agreed to hold the Alpha battle, and we have more visitors coming soon. I would like to hold the contest as soon as possible."

The Diego men exchanged looks and fidgeted awkwardly. It was Cadence again who stepped forward to answer, and Devin confirmed his own suspicions of who the next true Alpha of their pack was meant to be. "That shouldn't be a problem. None of us like having to have this battle at all, but it is the only fair way after everything that happened."

"Understood. Follow me." Devin shifted again and waited patiently while the Diego wolves stepped back to the tree line to collect their bags. They each threw a satchel over their neck, spinning it so it rested against their spine, and then shifted back into their animal form.

A nod from Cadence, and they were on their way back to the Alpha cabin. Devin wasn't quite sure what to make of them all, but he was willing to give them the benefit of the doubt. Sending his thoughts to his wife, he ran.

We're on our way back, sugar. There are ten of them just like we planned.

Good, I'm not sure we could manage more. Is it safe?

Yeah, I think so. Damon, what did you think?

Rolando is still bitter, but Diego's son Cadence isn't. He is clearly the current leader of their group.

I agree.

Well it sounds like you two have it all worked out. We'll be waiting at the big house for you. I've put together some food and drinks so they can relax when they get here.

When we finish getting them settled, I have plans for you, beautiful, so don't wear yourself out.

Instead of replying, Caroline just sent them a few wicked images for their minds to play with, and Devin happily doubled his speed. He needed to settle the Diego family in before he could disappear with her, but he wasn't opposed to rushing them.

The ladies of the Gray pack were able to obtain everything necessary to fill the three new residences. There were only ten wolves coming, but they had overprepared by building two cabins to house six wolves each, and one cabin for Cadence Diego and his second. Normally they wouldn't have made separate accommodations for a wolf until after he had won the Alpha position, but traditionally the son of the Alpha wolf would inherit his father's position when the reigning Alpha decided to step down.

In the case of the Diego pack, Barton had been killed in the most dishonorable way possible, attacking another wolf pack for personal vengeance. So the standard rules didn't apply. Every wolf in the pack who thought themselves strong enough would have the opportunity to fight in the Alpha battle. In Whitney's opinion, the tradition was archaic and disgusting, but the Diego wolves had voted to use the traditional system to determine their Alpha's rightful place.

It was expected that Cadence would still win his position of power, but there was an air of doubt when three other wolves had taken up the battle position. That meant that a total of four wolves would fight alongside their preselected seconds. Along with the eight contenders would be two of the pack's elders who would stand in for the majority of the pack as the judges of the battle.

In essence, the Gray pack was expected to do nothing but remain an impartial audience. It was odd, but it all came down to tradition. In order for the rest of the werewolf community to take the new Alpha seriously, they had to follow tradition.

The day after the shopping trip, Whitney found herself sitting on the sofa of her Alpha's cabin, nervously awaiting Devin and Damon's arrival with their guests. Tawny, Shandi, and Caroline were all just as fidgety. None of the women were allowed to join the Gray men in meeting the visitors at the edge of the den property. With so few of the strong Betas still at the den, Devin didn't want to take a chance on an ambush taking out both the male and female leaders of the pack. Most of the Gray wolves would meet the visitors later at the den clearing when Devin introduced them.

Whitney was in the middle of describing her new contract with a local wildlife magazine when the fragrance hit her straight in the gut. It swamped her senses so fully that she moaned out loud, drawing confused looks from her friends. She couldn't help it. The sharp scent of sandalwood filled her nostrils, fogging her brain. Her breath was trapped in her lungs, and her heart was racing. She could feel her wolf butting against her, trying desperately to get out, to find the origins of the deliciously enticing aroma. Her skin tingled all over, and even the tiny hairs on her neck stood up as it became stronger.

Twisting her head, she heard the crunch of feet on the grassy front lawn, followed by the rumble of male voices. Her body started trembling with anticipation, and it all clicked in her head in an instant. Her mate.

Mate.

Her heart pounded at the one word growled by her wolf, and she gasped as it bounced in her brain like a ping pong ball. Her mate was headed this way, and her wolf wanted him desperately. No, not wanted, that wasn't a strong enough word. She *needed* him. Her body ached with the need. She could feel the points of her canine teeth as they lowered, and her bones screamed out to shift and run toward the scent of her soul's other half.

The door pushed open and she heard a sharp male voice snarl, "Move, now." Devin and Damon came through it first as a growl escaped her throat that was matched by someone on the other side of the door.

Wait…was that two growls? What the hell was happening?

Before she could question it further, she was on her feet, moving toward the front door. Devin and Damon were forcibly pushed out of the doorway, and a pair of the sexiest and scariest looking men she had ever seen filled her vision.

Her pussy wept into her panties, and her nipples stood up hard as diamonds, begging to be touched. Her wolf whined with pleasure at being this close to its mate, but the human side of her brain was struggling, and her hands were trembling. Confusion hummed through her as her eyes darted back and forth between the two. They were the epitome of tall, dark, and handsome, but they both carried an aura of bad boy, too. Who was her mate? Shouldn't she just know?

Instead of moving closer, she took a step backward, away from the unknown. The two men growled simultaneously, and the slightly shorter of the two stalked toward her first, with the taller one right in his shadow.

In that moment, the fear of the unknown was overcome by an animalistic desire to be in her mate's arms, and she moved forward, meeting the first man in only a couple steps. He wrapped one arm around her waist and used the other hand to grip the nape of her neck, tilting her head backward. She felt her lips part as he dropped his head down. When their mouths met, she whimpered loudly in her throat, and her body caught fire. It raced through her system, lighting her soul up from the inside out, and she very nearly came in front of everyone.

His mouth was hard and forceful, but his tongue swept leisurely over hers in a sensual dance. Tempting and teasing while demanding and devouring. It was everything she had hoped to feel when she met her mate. She felt their souls touch as he held her, and she wanted to laugh, cry, and eat him alive all at the same time.

A second pair of hands touched her shoulders, and her wolf relaxed even further at this new touch. Her body responded by pressing back against his hardness. It was several moments before she grasped the fact that she was being held by two different men, and her wolf was ecstatic about both of them.

Roughly jerking her mouth free from the stranger's passionate onslaught, she panted, trying to recover her breath and her brain function. Two men meant two mates. Fuck no, her brain screamed at her, while her wolf rolled around inside her like a happy puppy.

Mate.

Stupid wolf. Was that the only word she knew now? She closed her eyes, trying to get her bearings before opening her mouth, but all she could hear was her wolf.

Mate. Mate. Mate.

"What the hell is going on?" Devin demanded from the doorway. She jumped, letting out a nervous whine before opening her eyes and looking up.

"Oh my God," she whispered as her vision was trapped by the darkest brown eyes she had ever seen in her life. They were the color of melted dark chocolate, and right now they were glowing. She could feel her own wolf under her skin basking in the heated gaze, but she fought to tamp it down. "Who are you? What is happening?"

"Exactly what the fuck I want to know." Her oldest brother Liam's voice came out in a snarl, but she couldn't tear her eyes away from the man still holding her close. A soft sigh against her ear and the tightening of fingers on her shoulders made her jump. The second man was still there, too.

"I'm Cadence Diego. But you already know what's happening, my flower. I'm your mate. Now, tell me your name." His voice soaked into her veins like aged whiskey, and she felt her body relaxing even further under his touch.

"Whitney Gray," she heard herself murmur in an unusually husky tone.

"*Whitney*…. beautiful." The second man's voice was lower and deeper than Cadence's, but it affected her equally. Her panties were so wet that she was afraid she was dripping on the carpet, and she clenched her thighs together. Both men let out a low rumble of approval as the strong scent of desire drifted around the three of them like a cloud. "I'm Mateo Diego, Whitney, and apparently you are also *my* mate."

She couldn't seem to form words with her tongue. It was as if the ground had just suddenly thrust her up in the air and then disappeared from beneath her, leaving her to free-fall back down to Earth. Liam broke the tension.

"Devin, do something! These two fuckers can't just waltz in here and screw my baby sister on the living room floor," Liam snarled. Whitney's eyes drifted over to the doorway and took in the fact that they had a rather large audience for this very private moment.

A sense of awkwardness filled her, and she pressed her hands against Cadence's chest, giving him a little push to get some distance. Drawing in a deep breath, she turned back to Liam. His ice-blue eyes were filled with an equal amount of anger and concern, and her heart squeezed. This was her big brother. She knew how much he wanted to protect her, but he was going about it the wrong way.

"Shut up, Liam. This isn't about you and what makes you uncomfortable. I just found my mate…er…mates. I think you should be congratulating me." Her tone was firm but not harsh.

A low chuckle had her turning to take in the man behind her. Mateo was about two inches taller than Cadence, which put him at six and a half feet tall. Compared to her five foot eight inches, they were mountains. Especially when she took in the ridges and mounds of muscle they were encased in. She had grown up around handsome faces and athletic bodies, but she couldn't help perusing their body builder physiques with feminine appreciation. They were both delicious looking men. Cadence joined his pack mate in soft laughter, and her pride prickled.

"Are you laughing at me?" Knowing she sounded snotty didn't stop the words from coming out, but it did stop her from pinning Mateo with a nasty glare. Especially when his eyes narrowed, and he stopped laughing.

"I would never laugh at you, mate. Don't misinterpret my admiration as arrogance, *mi reina*." The way the last word rolled off his tongue with the hint of a Spanish accent made her pussy clench.

"Well, this is certainly unexpected, Diego," Devin said from the doorway where he stood with his arms across his chest.

Cadence let out a sigh, and Whitney could have sworn she saw irritation flit through his dark eyes before he turned to respond. "Yes, it is, but as you can see, just like everyone else I am subject to nature. Whitney is very clearly my mate, and apparently my cousin's mate as well. I've never encountered a mating like this, so I'm not sure how we proceed." His body was tight with tension as he braced himself in front of her Alpha and her brother.

Whitney couldn't stop herself from reaching out to touch him. There was something inside her that just needed to soothe him. She stroked her fingers over the column of his neck from behind and flattened her hand against his back. The low rumble of approval and the press of his body backward against her palm confirmed that he took comfort in her touch and she nearly giggled with pleasure. Only her personal irritation at the odd urge of feminine flirtation stopped her.

"A mating like this? What do you mean?" Liam said sharply. He still looked ready to pounce on Cadence at any moment, and Whitney wanted to scream at him to back the fuck off.

"I've heard about ménage matings, but we haven't experienced any in our pack. Have you experienced them before?"

Devin and the others in the room laughed loudly while Liam continued to give Cadence and Mateo the stink eye.

"Experienced it? Oh yeah, we've definitely experienced it," Devin said. "Damon and I share our mate, Caroline, and our pack has one other triad that just mated. Two of our Betas found their mate and were married over the weekend. Rafe and Ryley are brothers as well."

"Hmm…I would say there is something in the water in Kansas City, but I've heard that the Stone pack in Texas is having many of these plural relationships, too."

Devin narrowed his light-green gaze and looked intrigued. "Really? I haven't spoken to Lafayette in more than a year, so I had no idea. This is something fairly new to our pack as well. Damon and I were the first pair to find ourselves mated to the same woman."

"Perhaps the ways of nature are not as permanent as you believe."

Everyone startled when a musical voice fell over them, and they turned as a group to watch the Gray pack sage, Delaky, enter the room from the back. She was the one person who could sneak up on a were-wolf. The only creature alive that seemed to move with absolute silence.

A tiny spit of a woman, Delaky was one of the most beautiful beings that Whitney had ever seen. She had always admired her long, white-blonde tresses that tumbled down her back well past her butt, and the way that her clear white skin glowed like moonlight on snow. If it weren't for her unnervingly odd way of pinpointing a person's thoughts, Whitney might have chosen to spend more time with her. But as it was, she had way too many things she preferred to keep private, so she avoided her at all costs.

Devin stepped forward and held his arm out, leading her toward the new threesome. "Delaky, this is Cadence and Mateo Diego. They are vying for the Alpha position in the Diego pack."

"Welcome, son of the moon. I can see the journey has been arduous."

Son of the moon? Whitney stared at Delaky blankly as Cadence reached a hand out to greet her. In true Delaky fashion, she turned it over and stared into his palm, tracing the line that life had carved into the skin. Cadence stood quietly, allowing the woman a moment to reflect. She smiled up at him and nodded. "Strong currents have aligned the moon with the sun nicely for you."

"Thank you, grandmother. The road has been long, and I was looking forward to a long rest, however now…" His rich brown eyes darted back up to meet Whitney's and again she struggled to breathe. There was a riot of emotions in his gaze, but desire burned deep, creating warmth in her chest that made her heart skip a beat.

"Yes, you have found your mate. Possibly a better path than the one you first started on, or perhaps an intersection in the path with two choices for the future?" Delaky turned to face Mateo without elaborating on her strange question. Her expression was serious, verging on harsh as she spoke to him. "The venom of a snake brought only pain into your soul, but scars can be healed, my child. Storms blow out like candles. Draw on the strength that is your gift, and then accept your failures. The broken can be mended."

Mateo's eyes widened and his fingers gripped Whitney's shoulders tightly. Delaky hadn't even looked at Mateo's palm, but clearly she was seeing something in him and his future that no one else knew. Was she also seeing his past? Whitney was suddenly feeling claustrophobic between the two large men. Stepping out from between them, she felt Mateo stiffen at her withdrawal.

"I hate to end this chat, but I think I need a moment to myself." She took another step away from the two strangers who made her blood boil without even trying. The sweet scent of her fear rose in the air around them. All this time she had been waiting for her perfect match, but never once did she consider that she might have two perfect pieces. What would it mean for her plans for the future? How could she possibly mate with two complete strangers? Her wolf fought inside her to get back to their side, but she continued to move away.

"Whitney—"

When Cadence would have moved toward her, Liam stepped between them. "No. She said she needed some space, and you'll give it to her."

Whitney didn't wait to see the outcome of the pissing match between her brother and the two men her life was destined for. Instead she turned and ran up the stairs and down the hallway, shutting herself in the small study that Devin used for pack business. With her back pressed to the closed door, she let her trembling body slump to the floor as she gasped for breath. Her body ached to be with two people she had never even laid eyes on until today, but her brain was screaming at her to fight it.

She just didn't know what to do.

This was so unlike her. She was known to have a well-laid path for her future. In fact, everyone teased her for being so meticulous about planning details that she sometimes felt she was unable to change her mind once a path was laid. Wasn't this an epic curveball for fate to throw her way?

Her mind drifted to the contract she had just accepted. It was for a three-page photo spread, each page representing a different animal that resided in the area. Wolves, foxes, and hawks. Drawing deep breaths, she focused in on what she needed to do to fulfill the contract. She began laying out her plans for obtaining the perfect shots, and by the time she had plotted all three photo shoots, she had managed to calm herself back down. It was her way of finding her center. If she knew what was to come, she could plan for it and handle it. It was the unknown that scared her the most.

When a loud knock finally came, she felt better prepared to handle it, and she stood on steady legs and flung the door open to face her future.

Purchase Caress of the Wolf at www.LoriKingBooks.com